KT-411-763

She was caught in his piercing gaze. 'Trust me. There's nothing more intimate on offer than that.'

Everything went very still. In the silence, Michelle became painfully aware of a sound inside her head. It was all her dreams, crumbling into dust.

'Unless,' he said slowly, 'you have something more intimate in mind…?'

His voice lilted with danger. Michelle sensed it. Her mother might have seen off all her boyfriends in the past, but when it came to Alessandro Castiglione no previous experience was necessary.

Their swing seat rocked gently in the warm breeze, scented by low-growing thyme. Michelle hoped it would cool her flaming cheeks. Instead she felt hotter than ever. She began moving uneasily. Strange feelings flowed through her body every time she looked at him.

His arm dropped lazily along the back of the bench. 'What's the matter, *cara*?'

She stood up quickly. 'I don't like this.'

He laughed. It was a low, provocative sound.

'No? I think you like it very much.'

Christina Hollis was born in Somerset, and now lives in the idyllic Wye Valley. She was born reading, and her childhood dream was to become a writer. This was realised when she became a successful journalist and lecturer in organic horticulture. Then she gave it all up to become a full-time mother of two, and to run half an acre of productive country garden. Writing Mills & Boon® romances is another ambition realised. It fills most of her time, between complicated rural school runs. The rest of her life is divided between garden and kitchen, either growing fruit and vegetables or cooking with them. Her daughter's cat always closely supervises everything she does around the home, from typing to picking strawberries!

Recent titles by the same author:

THE RUTHLESS ITALIAN'S INEXPERIENCED WIFE
HER RUTHLESS ITALIAN BOSS
ONE NIGHT IN HIS BED
COUNT GIOVANNI'S VIRGIN
THE ITALIAN BILLIONAIRE'S VIRGIN

THE TUSCAN TYCOON'S PREGNANT HOUSEKEEPER

BY
CHRISTINA HOLLIS

MILLS & BOON®

Pure reading pleasure™

DID YOU PURCHASE THIS BOOK WITHOUT A COVER?

If you did, you should be aware it is **stolen property** as it was reported *unsold and destroyed* by a retailer. Neither the author nor the publisher has received any payment for this book.

All the characters in this book have no existence outside the imagination of the author, and have no relation whatsoever to anyone bearing the same name or names. They are not even distantly inspired by any individual known or unknown to the author, and all the incidents are pure invention.

All Rights Reserved including the right of reproduction in whole or in part in any form. This edition is published by arrangement with Harlequin Enterprises II BV/S.à.r.l. The text of this publication or any part thereof may not be reproduced or transmitted in any form or by any means, electronic or mechanical, including photocopying, recording, storage in an information retrieval system, or otherwise, without the written permission of the publisher.

This book is sold subject to the condition that it shall not, by way of trade or otherwise, be lent, resold, hired out or otherwise circulated without the prior consent of the publisher in any form of binding or cover other than that in which it is published and without a similar condition including this condition being imposed on the subsequent purchaser.

® and TM are trademarks owned and used by the trademark owner and/or its licensee. Trademarks marked with ® are registered with the United Kingdom Patent Office and/or the Office for Harmonisation in the Internal Market and in other countries.

First published in Great Britain 2009
Harlequin Mills & Boon Limited,
Eton House, 18-24 Paradise Road, Richmond, Surrey TW9 1SR

© Christina Hollis 2009

ISBN: 978 0 263 87217 0

Set in Times Roman 10½ on 12¾ pt
01-0609-47818

Printed and bound in Spain
by Litografia Rosés, S.A., Barcelona

THE TUSCAN TYCOON'S PREGNANT HOUSEKEEPER

To all carers, everywhere

CHAPTER ONE

ANY MINUTE now! Michelle thought as the prow of the *Arcadia* nosed around the headland of St Valere. She had been waiting for this. Even so, she took a moment to admire her employer's vast yacht as it cut a white slit through the bright blue Mediterranean.

It would be a terrible wrench when this temporary job came to an end—if anyone could call being house-keeper at the villa Jolie Fleur 'work'. This position was a godsend, although the thought of her contract coming to an end lurked on her horizon like a big black cloud. And right now she was watching a thunderhead arrive to join it.

The previous day, her employer's domestic manager had rung Michelle from the yacht. Sounding tense and exasperated, the woman had warned her that an unex-pected guest was going to be staying at the villa. Michelle had soon found out why. One of her em-ployer's grandest guests was not fitting in to life on board ship. Michelle had laughed at this, thinking it was because of seasickness. But the truth was more than that.

Billionaire art dealer Alessandro Castiglione couldn't

be confined to the ocean. He was *supposed* to be taking a few weeks' complete break from work, the house-keeper had said, but her tone had told Michelle more than her words. She had known then what was in store for her, because she had seen plenty of men like him. Alessandro Castiglione would be a driven man, who drove his staff mad at the same time. He might be, as the woman had told her, 'The best-looking thing in every magazine!', but Michelle knew it took more than good looks to keep a tycoon at the top of his game.

Cleaning offices in central London had given her a glimpse of the brutal side of business life. So when the domestic manager had added a bit of gossip, Michelle had taken it with a pinch of salt. This man, she'd said, had recently taken over his father's firm and sacked nearly all its employees. If that wasn't bad enough, the woman had added in a low voice, they were all his aunts, uncles and cousins!

What sort of man would sack his relatives? Even Michelle's mother had never done that! She thought back to the life she had been so glad to abandon a few months earlier. Working for her mother had been hell. Mrs Spicer was an absolute perfectionist. The two of them, as Spicer and Co, had built up a reputation for fast, discreet domestic service anywhere in central London. Mrs Spicer had given the orders. Michelle had been the 'and Co' part of their business. She did all the dirty work.

But I'm in sole charge now! Michelle thought. De-spite her nervousness, she allowed herself a small smile as she waited to greet her famous house guest. However bad he was, Alessandro Castiglione couldn't possibly be a worse task-master than her mother.

Michelle always kept Jolie Fleur spotless, so this unexpected arrival hadn't made too much extra work for her. And what was the worst this man could do? Sack her? She only had a few weeks left in this position anyway. He might be an unexploded bomb, but Michelle had total confidence in her skills. She knew that if she worked hard and kept out of his way there would be no reason for him to lose his temper—at least not with her.

A man who dumps his own relatives will think nothing of throwing me out on my ear, and I'm not ready to leave! She thought. A keen sense of self-preservation had got her this far in life. Now she had escaped from England, she was curious to see how much further she might go.

As she watched from the clifftop overlooking the bay, a shape detached itself from the yacht's flight deck. It was a helicopter. Michelle shaded her eyes with her hand. It was always exciting to watch it swing into the hard blue sky with the grace of a wheeling seagull. She spent so long gazing up, the helicopter was almost overhead before she remembered she ought to be in position to welcome her unwelcome guest. She walked around to the front doors of the villa, making one last check of the exterior as she did so. The windows and white paintwork gleamed in the blinding sunlight. Inside the house, everything was ready. The caretaker and the gardener were the only permanent members of staff during the holiday season, but they weren't anywhere to be seen.

Nervously, she checked her fingernails and her uniform. Everything was clean and neat, as usual. Keeping busy was Michelle's way of coping with the world. With nothing left to panic about, she ran through what she would do when the unexpected house guest landed.

I'll give him a smile and a slight bow of my head, she thought. *Then I'll extend my hand for a handshake, tell him to ring me if he needs anything, and vanish.*

That didn't sound too difficult. The tricky part was actually managing it. Michelle loved this job because it gave her the chance to spend a lot of time on her own. People always made her nervous. The prospect of meeting a man who was apparently never photographed with the same model twice—woman or car—terrified her.

The incoming helicopter's rumble increased, until it vibrated right through her body. She looked down at the palms of her hands. Tiny beads of perspiration sparkled in their shallow creases. Absent-mindedly she ran them over the severe black skirt of her uniform and then stopped. A proper French chatelaine would never do such a thing!

I might be lucky and find he spends all his time out on the town, she thought, desperately trying to buoy up her spirits. *In that case he'll be nocturnal, so I'll hardly see him. Making his stay run smoothly will be enough for me.*

She walked quickly round to the front of the villa, the stiff sea breeze at her back. All the windows and doors were wide open, letting a cooling draught rush right through the house. Michelle thought the rich smell of the maquis was much nicer than the soulless scents pumped out by the air-conditioning system. Once she was in place, she could watch the helicopter land with a clear conscience. As it drew closer to the helipad, the racket of its rotors was almost too much to bear.

Michelle turned away from the sound and moved closer to the door for protection.

Turning around again, she expected to see the helicopter on the lawn. She got a surprise. It was still hanging in the air. Something must be wrong. Gaston, the pilot, was usually in such a tearing hurry to get back to his poker game on the yacht that he plonked the machine down anywhere. Smashed shrubs and crushed flowers were painful reminders of Gaston's previous overshoots and under-steering. Jolie Fleur's carefully tended mixed borders weren't so much a reminder of their English owner's homeland, they were more of a war zone.

This time was clearly going to be different. Michelle assumed there was a new pilot at the controls. Gaston would never take so long lining up his approach. But when the helicopter suddenly swung away and made a circuit of the house to try another approach, she caught sight of the pilot's face. It was the same old Gaston—but, from the furious look on his face, a perfectionist was schooling him in the art of landing.

By the time the helicopter finally came to rest, its skids were lined up exactly with the white letter 'H' stencilled in the centre of Jolie Fleur's main lawn. The racket had been deafening. Michelle's carefully brushed hair was blown to a thatch. As she tried to tame her mousy brown tangle, disaster struck. The helicopter's rotors slowed and its downdraught eased. The drop in pressure meant a gust of wind off the sea got behind the villa's door and slammed it shut behind her with a thunderous bang. Michelle jumped—or would have done, if her uniform hadn't held her back. Its skirt had been sucked in between the heavy door and its jamb. She was trapped and could hardly move.

Tugging at it with growing horror, she realised this was the first and only low point since she'd left England—but it was bottomless. She knew the door would have locked.

Desperately hoping for a miracle, she tried the handle anyway. The door didn't move. Her guardian angel must be on holiday.

Michelle's pulse had been galloping with nerves all morning. Now it went into overdrive. What could she do? Wave hopefully at the tall, rangy figure unfolding itself from the helicopter? Appealing for help to a guest when she was supposed to be so efficient wouldn't be the best start to their working relationship. Someone who could teach precision to a slap-dash pilot in one lesson was unlikely to have any time for accidents or mishaps.

Desperately, she tried working her skirt out through the crack, pulling it up and down, backwards and forwards. Nothing worked. The alternative was to tear herself free, leaving her skirt behind. That wasn't an option. A careless housekeeper was one thing. A half-dressed one was unforgivable—and totally unforgettable. Trussed up like a chicken, she resigned herself to a roasting.

Signor Alessandro Castiglione stood on the parched lawn, his back to her, as he waited for his designer luggage to be unloaded. Michelle watched, getting hotter and hotter. Long, agonising seconds dripped away. She tensed, ready with a million explanations. Taking possession of a briefcase and laptop, her guest left Gaston to deal with everything else. Marching towards the house, he covered the distance in a terrifyingly short time.

He was nothing like as old as she'd expected, but to think such a young man was already notorious in the newspapers somehow made her situation much worse. Michelle's spirits skidded along rock-bottom. Despite his hunched shoulders and considered pace, he was moving quickly. Instead of taking the track of scuffed, dead grass leading directly from the helipad to the house, he took a much longer route. This went by way of paved paths through banks of thyme and sage, and stretched out her agony still further. Watching bees working among the herb flowers always persuaded Michelle to relax and linger. They had absolutely no effect on this man. He was totally single-minded. Looking neither to left nor right, he homed straight in on the front door of the villa.

If Michelle hadn't been so frantic she would have appreciated his fine features. The natural curl in his thick, dark hair, his quick brown eyes, frowning brow and heavy tread would normally have made such an impression on her she would have been struck dumb. Instead she was speechless with embarrassment. Hands behind her back, she went on easing, tugging and wheedling at her skirt to try and free it. It was no use.

The closer the newcomer got, the more frantic she felt. Her fingers throbbed from trying to break free. So did her pulse. It was so hot. She might as well have been a butterfly beating its wings against a closed window. She was well and truly stuck. If that wasn't bad enough, she was beginning to see why this guest hadn't fitted in on Mr Bartlett's yacht. It was designed for holidays and having a good time. Alessandro Castiglione looked as though he didn't know the meaning of the words. Despite the heat, he was wearing a top-quality suit and a hand-finished shirt. His only concessions to the Mediterranean were the ivory colour of his linen trousers and jacket, the open buttons at his neck, and the mulberry-coloured tie peeking from his pocket.

Michelle swallowed hard. The time for practising her welcome was over. Now for it…

'*Buongiorno*, Signor Castiglione. My name is Michelle Spicer, and I'll be looking after you during your stay here at Jolie Fleur.'

His pale, aristocratic face was compressed. 'I don't need looking after. That's why I jumped ship. There were too many people running round after me. All they do is get in my way,' he growled in faultless English, speaking with the accent of a Caesar. It drove everything from Michelle's mind except her fear of explaining exactly how much of a fool she was.

And then, ten feet away from her, his expression changed from distracted to thoughtful. He stopped. Michelle tried to take a step backwards away from him, but her heels rattled against the firmly closed door. There was no escape. She stood and quailed, while he stood and watched her. He pressed his lips together in a tight line, matching the deep furrows on his brow. Michelle couldn't think of a single thing to say. This was worse than she had ever imagined it would be. She was pinned to the door by his unblinking stare. Michelle tried to tell herself this was just another job and she really shouldn't care what impression he was getting of her. The truth was, she cared very much.

Staff should be invisible and silent. Here she was, pegged out with no hope of release. You couldn't get much more visible than that.

Why does he have to be so good-looking? she thought. *It wouldn't be half so bad if he was old, or ugly, or ranted and raved at me—anything would be easier to bear than this slow, silent interrogation…*

'Well! What have we got here?' he drawled eventually. 'You're trapped.'

So tell me something I don't know! she thought, but the relish in his eyes was too obvious. Instead, she nodded and tried to smile.

'I—I'm the housekeeper here at Jolie Fleur and I shall be doing everything I can to make your stay as pleasant as possible…' *Though how I'm going to manage it from here…* she added silently.

It didn't seem much of an obstacle to Alessandro Castiglione. He pinned her to the door with a knowing look.

'Everything?' he questioned with a mischievous twinkle. 'You mean my wish is your command? That's dangerous talk, *signorina*, when you look to be stuck fast!'

Michelle burbled something wordless, her mind melted by flames of embarrassment. She needn't have bothered. He was far too interested in her problem.

'I was trapped too—on that damned boat,' he added, almost sympathetically.

After a moment's hesitation, Michelle screwed up all her courage and tried an explanation.

'The door slammed shut in the helicopter's down-draught. The key is in my pocket, but I can't reach it,' she said, in a voice so small she hardly recognised it.

To her surprise he gave a quick nod of understanding. 'You must be more careful. This is a very heavy door, Michelle. You're lucky it's only your dress. You might have lost your fingers.'

Her heart slowed to about five hundred beats a minute. Looking into those *nocciola*-brown eyes was having a very strange effect on her. None of the bad things she had been told about him mattered any more. This was a man who had been through a lot. She could see that from his face. He must be in his late thirties, and creases etched between his brows added to the character of his otherwise fine features, but to Michelle he was at his loveliest when he smiled.

'My keys—' she tried to say, but no sound came out. Clearing her throat as delicately as she could, she tried again. 'My keys are in my pocket, but I can't reach them.'

'Then it's easily fixed,' he said as he moved towards her.

The villa's overhanging eaves meant she was imprisoned in the shade, but her temperature began to rise. The closer Alessandro got, the better-looking he became. Any lines on his face now were drawn by concentration. His aura of confidence should have put her at her ease, but it had exactly the opposite effect. There was nowhere for Michelle to look except straight at him. She was swept into the steady depths of his eyes and could study them all she liked. Alessandro Castiglione was far too busy to notice. He was concentrating on her waist.

'Surely if you were to turn around—?'

'How? I'm stuck!'

'I'll show you.'

He closed in on her until they were almost touching. She gazed up at him, her hazel eyes wide with anxiety. He placed his hands on her shoulders, and she flinched.

'Michelle! Anyone would think I was a monster.' He laughed.

'I'm sorry,' she muttered.

'Don't worry. I've had my quota of virgins for the day.' With that, he turned her—not to the left, as she'd imagined, but to the right. Now she was facing the door. She couldn't see him any more, but hardly needed to. The mere presence of him was sending out enough vibrations to tell her he meant business.

'That's given you more room to play with, hasn't it?' he asked in his deep brown voice.

Michelle tried, struggled and failed.

'Yes, but it's not enough. I still can't get my hand around into my pocket.'

The fragrance of his new clothes and expensive cologne retreated a little, but then returned with full force.

'How about if I try?'

Michelle nodded. His hand slid over her, and she was spellbound. His touch was slow and measured. Michelle felt it like a caress. She tried to steady her breathing. It was impossible. The air filling her lungs was superheated with his clean, understated fragrance.

'No—please—don't do that...' Michelle's protest sounded feeble and fake, even to her.

Alessandro's hand stopped moving, but he didn't take it away. She felt the warmth of it burning through the thin fabric of her uniform like a brand.

'What is it, Michelle?'

His rich accent made even those few simple words sound beautiful.

Michelle pressed her cheek hard against the impassive face of the front door and tried to keep cool. It wasn't easy when she could feel every one of his fingers.

'Nothing.' She shook her head.

Only, it's the first real time I've been touched by a man, she thought to herself.

The tips of his fingers slid lazily over her, searching. When he found what he was looking for, she gasped. His hand slid into her pocket and closed over her key fold.

'Now…I'm afraid I shall have to move in a lot closer to reach the keyhole…'

Michelle couldn't speak. He was leaning against her as he searched for the lock. The feel of his breath on her hair was intoxicating enough. When his right hand slid around her waist the breath caught in her throat. There was a click, and the door swung open. His supporting hand fell away from her and he stood back.

'You're free,' he said, nodding towards the entrance hall, smiling. It lit up his face, and she couldn't help pausing in wonder. Then a breeze rippled around them, bringing her situation right back to life again. She flung out her hand to stop the door slamming a second time. Alessandro's hand was already there. Electricity crackled right through her body. She felt his firm, warm fingers again—then snatched hers away.

'Thank you, Signor Castiglione. I'll show you to your suite. Then I'll take you on a tour of Jolie Fleur—' she gabbled, desperate to prove how capable she was.

'No—I'll be fine.' Alessandro cut her off. 'There's no reason why you should worry about me. Go and do whatever you have to. I'm more than capable of finding my way around a house alone.'

'Of course, Signor Castiglione.'

Michelle dipped her head politely and reversed away from him.

'Where are you going?'

'I'm going to change—this dress is all creased now. I live in the studio house. It's in the grounds, just over there.'

He frowned. 'Why don't you live in the main house?'

'I'm only temporary staff, *signor*. Given my position, I don't really fit in anywhere up at the house.'

'But Terence Bartlett told me his house was deserted—there must be plenty of spare rooms. All his staff are with him on the yacht. That's the only reason I got him to drop me off here, rather than heading for home. I employ even more people than he does,' he said, with a voice full of feeling.

Michelle wondered if this was before or after the re-dundancies, and shivered.

'To be honest, I prefer living away from the main house, *signor*. I like my own company, so the studio is ideal for me.'

'Do you mean the artist's studio?' he said slowly.

She nodded. 'There's a lot of equipment and things stored in there, *signor*, but none of it has been used or even opened.'

'Terence had it built so he could dabble, but he's never had the time to use it. Or the talent,' he added re-gretfully. 'Is it a good building?'

'It's wonderful, *signor*.' Michelle smiled.

Living in a place where works of art might one day

be made was another reason why she loved Jolie Fleur. The place was so beautiful it cried out to be drawn or painted. She wished she had one percent of the equipment that was lying abandoned in the apartment she was using. Then she reminded herself none of it was any use to her, as she lacked the nerve to try.

'May I take a look inside this studio of yours?'

How could she refuse? Alessandro was the boss, after all. She nodded. The idea of a man intruding into her personal space would normally set her teeth on edge. And yet something about *this* man made agreeing to his request the most natural thing in the world. She didn't want to cross him, but that wasn't the only reason. In the few minutes since he'd landed Michelle had realised something. He might be used to the company of stars and billionaires, but Alessandro Castiglione was the most natural, unaffected person she had ever met. He didn't waste words, either. That was something else in his favour. She much preferred an employer who kept quiet and let her get on with things, although the magnetic Signor Castiglione was bound to be quite a challenge. But Michelle knew her place. It was his holiday: her job was to keep him happy while keeping out of his way.

She found herself wondering whether he would be spending much time at the villa, or whether he would be travelling farther afield. And, whatever he did, would he have company? She began to think that keeping an invisible watch on this gorgeous man might be a lot more fun than hiding away from him completely…

CHAPTER TWO

MICHELLE'S heart leapt each time she saw her temporary home. It nestled in a sheltered part of the garden,
and was designed so that the banks of flowers billow-
ing on every side could be enjoyed whatever the weather. Glass made up most of the front of the building,
while deep eaves shaded a swing-seat. Michelle
unlocked the sliding French doors and stood aside for
him to go in.

'This is impressive.' Alessandro Castiglione looked
around the living room, with its stacks of art boxes and
storage bins. Wandering into the kitchen, he nodded appreciatively at the big stainless steel sink and double
drainers that took up most of the room. 'It wouldn't take
long to remove this partition wall to make better use of
the space,' he murmured to himself.

Michelle stood silently in a corner while he roamed
around, occasionally taking something from the huge
collection of equipment and supplies she had to
squeeze around. Once he had studied a packet of paper,
a box of pencils, an easel or some brushes, he put them
back carefully in their place. Michelle was glad to see
that. Most employers would have put them anywhere.

They pay you to be tidy for them, her mother had always said.

She found it fascinating to watch him when she could. Each time he caught her doing it, he smiled. Michelle found herself blushing madly, and had to look away. Her guest knew exactly the effect he was having.

'I never knew Terence had so many art books!' He ran his finger along the spines lining the shelves, but it was a volume open on the coffee table that really caught his eye. 'Raphael. He's one of my favourites. Do you mind if I borrow this one and take it back to the villa with me?'

He picked it up and began flicking through the pages, from the back to front of the book. Of all the ones to choose... Michelle felt as though he had reached inside her ribcage and pulled out her heart. She knew exactly what he was thinking, because she had experienced it so often herself. As he revelled in the beautiful pictures and glowing colours, it showed clearly in his face. It was only when he reached the flyleaf that he stopped smiling.

'"Presented to Michelle Spicer as part of the Lawrence Prize for the year's outstanding portfolio,"' he read aloud, and then looked at her directly. His eyes were smiling, 'So this is yours?'

Michelle nodded, too struck by the sparkle in his eyes to speak.

'A little light bedtime reading?'

'It's a bit too heavy for that, *signor.*'

'For one person, maybe...although two might manage, I suppose. One could read while the other looks on?'

A vision of Alessandro Castiglione in bed came to

Michelle, and it didn't involve any art books. She managed not to gasp aloud, but couldn't help taking a step backwards, away from him.

When he put her presentation book down on the table again Michelle was puzzled.

'Aren't you going to take it after all, *signor*?'

He shook his head. 'I couldn't possibly. It's yours and must mean so much to you.'

'It does—but if you want it…'

'Thank you. I'll let you have it back as soon as possible.' Taking possession of it again with relish, he patted the cover. 'This must be an inspiring place to work for you, as an artist. How many pictures have you done while you've been here?'

'None, *signor*. There's always too much work to do.'

He laughed politely, and brandished her book. 'Where's your portfolio now? You haven't got it here by any chance?'

Michelle clenched her teeth at the memory. The words had to struggle out.

'It got burned, *signor*.'

'I'm sorry.'

He sounded genuinely touched. 'I would have liked to have seen it. Never mind. I won't be a demanding guest. You'll have plenty of time for your art while I'm in residence here.'

He was right. Over the next few days Michelle found she actually had some spare time. It was unheard of. The Bartlett family were always thinking of bits and pieces that they'd forgotten to get delivered for their stay. Without having to drive into town several times a day,

Michelle could open her own art box for the first time since arriving in France.

Her efforts at sketching around the estate weren't very successful. Each time she caught sight of Alessandro she hid her sketchbook in case he wanted to look at her work. She couldn't bear showing her pictures to anyone. The only reason she had won the Lawrence Prize was because a tutor had entered Michelle's portfolio without her knowledge.

She was surprised at how often she bumped into Alessandro around the estate. He always smiled at her, and they often swapped a few words of polite, mean-ingless conversation. Michelle was intrigued. The Bartlett family and their other guests spent all their time indoors, bent over computer screens or mobile phones. Alessandro seemed to like fresh air as much as she did.

Once the ringing of his mobile phone joined the rustle of grasshoppers and the chirrup of birds echoing through the dusty landscape. Then it fell silent. It was only when Michelle went to fetch some water for the houseplants that she found out why. A state of the art PDA was lying in the bottom of the soft water tank. Pulling it out, she dried it off as best she could and rushed to find him. The red 'do not disturb' light was showing on the console beside the door of his suite, so she left the soggy device there without knocking. An hour later, Alessandro sought her out as she arranged flowers for the music room.

'I have something for the trash.' Taking her hand, he put the PDA in her palm and carefully closed her fingers around it. 'They say I need a break. Now I've had a few days' rest, I'm inclined to agree with them.'

All the time he was pressing her hand between both of his. It brought back memories of his touch gliding over her body as he'd searched for her keys. His grip was warm and reassuringly firm. In contrast to the grating tension in his voice when he'd arrived, his speech was now softer and lilting. He was so different from the hard-bitten workaholic she had been expecting that Michelle laughed out loud.

'You can't throw this away! It must have cost a fortune!'

'Michelle, it will not work now it has got wet. It's been nothing but a curse to me.'

Looking into the turbulence of his eyes, she could believe it. In that moment her heart went out to him. 'Don't worry, *signor*. I'll take care of it.' She smiled.

When he smiled back, it illuminated his face in a way that stopped Michelle's heart. Alessandro Castiglione was gorgeous, and he was smiling at her…

Alessandro wasn't someone to be tiptoed around, like her usual boss. He was much more approachable, but his reputation still haunted her, so she kept out of his way. All the same, every tiny sound made her glance up in case it was him. She found herself looking out for him all the time. When they passed in a corridor he'd smile at her. That simple gesture made up for the hours of worry she had endured before he arrived.

Michelle kept herself busy around the villa, which helped stop her daydreaming. But after work, when she got back to her silent apartment, her mind always went into overdrive. She'd relive every single moment of his arrival. The touch of his hands on her as he searched for her pocket. His firm grasp when he supported her as he opened the door… And, more than anything else, his beautiful dark eyes with their long, dense lashes. She tried to distract herself by getting out paper and pencils and sketching. But although she sat outside, intending to draw the garden, her pencil kept trying to catch Alessandro's likeness instead.

One evening, strangely dissatisfied, she decided on an early night. Sleep was impossible. The memory of him filled her off-duty hours as easily as he touched every moment of her working day.

It was long after midnight before she gave up trying to get to sleep. Staggering blearily into the studio house's kitchen, she made herself a cup of tea. Comfort eating was the only way to distract herself from thoughts of her delicious employer—or at least push him to the back of her mind—so, grabbing a packet of biscuits, she headed back to her bedroom. One look at the tangled bedclothes was enough to put her off. She decided to take her guilty pleasure out onto the veranda.

Unlocking the studio's French doors, she opened them wide. The night air was still, and fragrant with flowers. Stepping out into the dusky garden was like the first welcome of a deliciously cool swimming pool. She shivered at the thrill. It was a perfect night with no moon; every star was visible above the darkness of the estate.

'Buona sera, Michelle.' Alessandro's voice came to her, soft and low through the dusk.

She whirled around. He was leaning back lazily on the swing-seat outside her apartment, a glass in his hand. Immediately she tried to cover herself with her hands, conscious that the sliver of satin and lace she was wearing was hardly decent enough to wear in front of a guest—especially *this* guest!

'Would you like to join me for a drink, Michelle?' He picked up a bottle of wine from the table beside him and filled his glass. Holding it out to her, he watched her hesitant approach with a smile.

'Me?' she breathed.

'I don't see anyone else around.'

'But—but I can't! I'm not dressed…'

'You look fine to me.' His smile flashed very white in the soft glow filtering through the studio's curtains. 'I couldn't sleep, and came out looking for some fresh air. Was there ever a country estate with fewer places to sit? Don't the Bartletts *use* this place?'

Michelle shook her head. 'They prefer their computers. Guests are sometimes shown around before dinner, but apart from that I've usually got the gardens to myself.'

He chuckled. It was a soft, intimate sound, perfectly in tune with the warm dusk. 'I never expected *you* to venture out here after dark. You seem so quiet and reserved.'

'I love it out here, and it's perfectly safe.'

'That's not surprising. The security lights around the villa are triggered by every step. When I was walking on the terrace I felt as though I was in a Broadway production. I wanted somewhere relaxing.'

He was wearing an open-necked shirt, as perfectly white as the one he had arrived in. It shone like nicotiana flowers against the gloom, but the fragrance of him was altogether more sexy. It combined male musk with an elusive cologne that was expensively discreet.

Michelle's fingers clenched on the condensation-frosted glass in her hand. It wasn't enough to cool her thoughts.

She took a sip of her drink and coughed, not accustomed to the champagne bubbles.

'Champagne is my secret vice.' He chuckled, and as they sat back the atmosphere relaxed. 'I met the gardener this afternoon. He's very proud of the estate's strawberries. When they didn't appear on the menu this evening, I engaged in a little private enterprise and picked some for myself. Can you think of any better way to make the best of a sleepless night?'

Michelle shook her head. Her eyes were becoming more accustomed to the dark. Now she could see there was a dish on the table, too. He took a few berries from it and dropped them into her glass of champagne. Each one made a loud plop and an indulgent fizz in the stillness.

'The perfect finishing touch,' he murmured, watching her.

As she raised the slender glass to her lips she wrinkled her nose with pleasure at the rich aroma of ripe fruit and vintage wine. He smiled. Women were one of his greatest pleasures, but Miss Michelle Spicer was unlike any girl he had met before. She was as refreshing as a glass of ice-cold Vernaccia. He watched her, and knew that drinking champagne must be a rarity for her, from the way that half-smile danced across her face each time she took a sip.

She had completely forgotten the low cut of her nightdress, and the way its bias-cut satin clung to the rise of her breasts. Only a woman who spent too much time studying the form of other things could be so unaware of her own beauty. Alessandro knew a lot of women.

They all played on the effect they could have on a man. By contrast, Michelle seemed totally innocent.

'You eat the strawberries when they've had time to marinate in the champagne.'

Michelle smiled and popped one of the ripe berries into her mouth. The strawberries were like no others she had ever tasted. There were as soft and sweet as an angel's kiss. The thought made a connection in her mind.

As they sat together in the warm night, she looked across at Alessandro shyly. His profile was stunning as he looked up at the wide sky full of stars. In her mind, his lips promised beautiful words, spoken just for her. More than that, she fantasised about the touch of them against her skin. Sitting next to him like this was a fragile bubble of happiness. The gentle chorus of insects, the cool breeze on her skin, and the perfume of ripening fruit and flowers all added to the magic. Not even a bat, arriving to flicker around the heliotropes, could destroy this moment.

Alessandro looked to see if she was affected by it, and chuckled. 'Strawberries, champagne and a stranger after midnight—you're taking it all in your stride, Michelle,' he teased her gently.

There was a bitter-chocolate quality about his voice that sent a tremor right through Michelle's body. He noticed.

'You're cold—*dannazione*! If I'd brought my jacket I'd offer it to you. Why don't you go inside and fetch something?'

'I don't have anything,' she replied, hoping he would believe her. This was all too precious to spoil.

'Then sit closer to me. I can shield you from any chill.'

'I'm not cold.' *Not any more*, she thought, taking in a long, slow breath.

She wondered what to do if he insisted she moved nearer to him. Torn between doing the right thing and imagining how wonderful the wrong thing would be, she was tense with indecision. Then the fragrance of night stole over her. Sultry top notes of lavender and jasmine were lightened by the sweet, more elusive scent of roses. For Michelle, this was a dream come true. With nothing to do but enjoy her surroundings, she began to lose herself in fantasy.

'This is what I imagine a real English country garden would be like,' she said eventually.

'Then you are homesick, Michelle?'

'Oh, I'm so sorry, *signor*! I didn't mean to say that out loud.'

'Don't worry about it.' His voice was a low, seductive sound, steady against the background crackle of insects. 'And, as I shall be calling you Michelle, you should call me Alessandro.'

When he said that, she tensed, concentrating on the strawberries clustered at the bottom of her glass. He handed her a solid silver teaspoon. One by one she spooned them out, savouring every mouthful and every moment.

'You didn't answer my question, Michelle. *Are* you homesick?'

'No, not at all—unless you count being sick of home.' She stopped, remembered that part of her life was over, and smiled. 'Although I've put all that behind me now. I'm a free agent.'

She saw him raise his eyebrows and rushed to explain.

'That is—I mean—I don't have a home in England any more. And I never did manage to get my wish of a lovely little house like this, with roses around the door.'

'This isn't a house, it's a studio—and one I was hoping to use,' he said softly.

Michelle was quick to pick up on the tinge of regret in his voice. 'You can work from the house, *signor*—'

He shot her a warning look and she corrected herself, 'I mean, *Alessandro*. You should have let me show you around. The whole house is set up as a satellite office. It's got everything—'

He silenced her with a raised hand. 'This is all I need at the moment—some peace and quiet. Tonight I want to drink in this atmosphere and the starlight.'

He gestured towards the sky. Michelle lifted her eyes, following his finger as it pointed upwards. With the coast behind them, they were looking out over the velvety blackness of the villa's estate. Beyond its boundary walls lay miles of lavender fields and patches of undeveloped maquis. There were no disco lights to outshine the stars as they twinkled like pinpricks across the deep indigo of the night.

'Have you ever seen anything so beautiful, Michelle?' he asked.

She shook her head, although she thought *he* was more wonderful than anything else on show that night. Her emotions were in meltdown. Part of her wanted him to say more. Seduction would have been extra-sweet in this heavenly setting under the stars. Yet a spider's web of warnings tugged at her, holding her back.

Her mother had always told her how untrustworthy men could be. None had stuck around for long after they'd met the fearsome Mrs Spicer, that was for sure. The result was that Michelle couldn't fully enjoy the experience of being alone with such a wonderful man in this tempting situation. She was too busy watching for warning signs.

But if Alessandro realised how tense she was, he made no allowance for it.

'I think this has been the most miraculous evening I've ever experienced.' He took the champagne glass and spoon from her hands. Smiling, he saluted her with it. 'Thank you for sharing it with me.'

Michelle was stunned. No one had ever said anything like that to her before. 'If there's ever anything you want, Alessandro, you only have to ask,' she whispered.

He put the glass down on the table behind him.

'That's dangerous talk, Michelle.' There was a provocative look in his eyes that almost stopped her heart. 'But…if you're sure you don't mind…perhaps you could do me a favour?'

'What is it?' she asked—much too quickly.

His expression moved slowly but surely into a wide, tempting smile.

'How would you feel about moving into the villa while I'm staying here?'

CHAPTER THREE

MICHELLE gazed at him, totally unable to form any words. Alessandro leaned forward a little, adding mischeviously, 'I can guess how wicked it will make you feel, but don't worry. We'll keep it our secret. No one need know.'

That forced Michelle to find her voice. 'What are you saying?' Blushing, she lowered her head. Silence closed in around her. When she looked up again, his understanding smile set her tingling from head to foot.

'I want to use your studio for my art. I know you like to keep your distance from the rest of the indoor staff, but there's no one here right now. You could move in for a while and give me free rein.' She was caught in his piercing gaze. 'Trust me. There's nothing more intimate on offer than that.'

Everything went very still. In the silence, Michelle became painfully aware of a sound inside her head. It was all her dreams crumbling into dust.

'Unless,' he said as an afterthought, 'you have something more intimate in mind...?'

His voice lilted with danger. Michelle sensed it. Her mother might have seen off all her boyfriends in the past, but when it came to Alessandro Castiglione no previous experience was necessary. This man was seduction in the flesh.

Pressing his foot into the carpet of tiny sweet herbs beneath the swing-seat, he set it moving. It rocked gently in the warm breeze, scented by low-growing thyme. Michelle hoped it would cool her flaming cheeks. Instead, she felt hotter than ever. She began moving uneasily. Strange feelings flowed through her body every time she looked at him. She had never experienced anything like this before. At home, eye contact had been something to be avoided. Here, held by his steady gaze, it was to be enjoyed.

His arm dropped lazily along the back of the bench. Michelle had an overwhelming urge to lean against it. She had felt the strong security of his hands once already. To feel them a second time, in a caress rather than as a support, would be heavenly. It took a real effort to shake free from the power of his eyes.

'What's the matter, *cara*?'

She stood up quickly. 'I don't like this.'

He laughed. It was a low, provocative sound.

'No…? I think you like it very much.'

Michelle couldn't answer. Telling the truth at a time like this would only catapult her straight into trouble.

'Tonight belongs to you and me, Michelle. There are no spectators, no listeners behind doors. We are free to be ourselves for once.'

He looked her up and down with a practised eye. She felt like a rabbit, cornered by a very attractive fox. She sat down again, faintly surprised by her new courage. A slow smile warmed his eyes. He stretched out his limbs, extending his legs across the gravel in front of the studio house. His body language and his expression were so open and inviting. He looked a completely different man from the world-weary professional who had stamped up to the villa a few days earlier.

Michelle caught her breath. He was wonderful. *Wonderfully dangerous*, she reminded herself. Something about that look in his eyes warned her to take care. She was only the hired help, after all. She would be mad to encourage him. He had burst into her life from nowhere, and he would vanish with the same speed.

A mischevious breeze ruffled his night-dark hair.

'Would you like some more champagne, *signor*?' she said, before he could draw her further into his orbit.

He shook his head, and she pursed her lips. He must think she was a complete innocent, talking about wine when there might be so much more on offer. It was a short step from that to imagining she was stupid. Michelle knew that wasn't true—despite the number of times her mother had said it.

'So—what's your answer?' he went on. 'Will you move out of here so I can indulge myself in Terence's purpose built art studio? The change would do us both a lot of good. Trust me,' he repeated.

Michelle sensed it was the last thing she should do. On the other hand…she needed to prove she wasn't a naïve fool. Alessandro had looked so careworn when he'd arrived. He already looked a lot better. How much more improvement might there be if she gave in to him over this little matter? Music was supposed to work wonders as a form of therapy. Art might do the same for him.

'All right,' she agreed, before she could change her

mind. But she knew his reputation couldn't be allowed to frighten her into falling in with all his plans. She was determined to have boundaries.

'Good…you're making a work-worn billionaire very happy.' He laughed softly.

Michelle could tell he hadn't said it to pull rank. His words had been hollow, and his gaze told of something deeper behind his words. Michelle shivered, and he snapped out of his reverie.

'You *are* cold. I can't keep you from your bed any longer, Michelle. I must go.' He stood up and, bending forward until his head was almost touching hers, took her hand and raised it to his lips. His parting kiss was the light touch of a butterfly dancing on her skin, but it burned like the passion that fuelled his life.

'*Buona notte*, Michelle. Sweet dreams,' he added with a flash of mischief as he swung away into the night.

Michelle watched him move away through the shadowy garden. His white shirt was visible for a long way, despite the gloom. It only disappeared when he closed the villa door behind him. It extinguished the last hold he had over her. Standing up, she went slowly into the studio house. How could she have been so wrong about him? Although there was no doubt that beneath his handsome exterior Signor Alessandro Castiglione was ruthless, tonight he had been devastatingly charming. She drifted back into the studio house in a daze.

Michelle set her alarm clock for 4:00 a.m., but was awake in time to switch it off. It would have echoed through the peace and quiet of the Jolie Fleur estate. The memory of Alessandro's midnight visit was still hot in her mind.

It took her no time at all to pack. When she had stacked her few possessions on the doorstep of the studio house, she showered and then dressed in her bikini. It had been a long night, with not enough sleep. A swim before breakfast would perk her up. Dawn in the garden was as magical as dusk, and she could hardly wait to experience it again. She pulled on her dressing gown for the short walk to the villa's outdoor pool. The sun was still low, and filtered by a slight sea mist.

Leaving her studio apartment for the last time, she immersed herself in the chilly dawn. Rounding the hedge sheltering the pool she stopped and stared. Alessandro was already in the water, moving through it as though he owned the element.

'*Buongiorno*, Michelle.' He raised a hand to her. Water cascaded from his long, muscular limbs. He swam to the side of the pool in a few strokes. Folding his arms on the edge, he looked up at her appreciatively.

'The water is cold, but this is a great way to kick-start your system first thing in the morning. Come on in.'

'Er…no, thanks. I'm not here to swim. I—I only came for a walk around the grounds.'

Alessandro threw himself backwards in a creamy foam of water. Michelle knew only too well where to look, but didn't. The temptation was unbearable, but she tried to act as though muscular men stripped down to their Speedos were an everyday part of her life.

'If you didn't come to swim, why are you wearing that bikini?'

Michelle dropped her attention to the tiles at her feet. As she did so, she saw that the ties of her dressing gown had worked loose during her headlong dash to the pool.

Wrapping it tightly around herself, she secured it with a firm knot.

Alessandro slid through the water like a seal to take up a position at the side of the pool again. Heat flared in Michelle's cheeks. She went over in her mind everything that had gone on between them the night before. The embarrassment had all been on her side, the easy charm on his. As she burned, she wished with all her heart she could come up with some wonderful remark. Anything—*anything*—to recapture the magic of last night…

'So? What are you waiting for? Join me.'

She twiddled the tie of her dressing gown. 'I couldn't possibly…I only work here. You're a guest.'

'And I'm only inviting you into the water. There's no rule that says staff can't come in with me, is there?' He shrugged.

With her body reacting to everything Alessandro had on show, Michelle didn't know what to do. Instinct told her to take a chance, but her sense of decency said *run*. She stared down at a ladybird creeping across the tiled surround of the pool. It was heading for her toes with the sort of determination she desperately needed.

'I'm sorry, Alessandro,' she said, with more truth that he could ever have imagined. 'It's not my place.'

He was floating on his back, watching her. When she said that, he stood up in a shower of droplets. Michelle's eyes were instantly riveted on him. She couldn't tear them away. He looked magnificent. Two metres of tightly packed muscles and smooth, flawless skin. He had the pale colouring of someone who spent all day behind a desk, but who would toast to a golden tan in no time at all. Michelle was imagining the effect already. Tiny trickles of water led her gaze down over his bunched pectorals and his flat, muscular belly.

Laughing at her expression, when he said his next words he gave her exactly the push she needed.

'If you're determined to be a member of staff, then I'll stick to the rules too. I'm going to give you a direct order. It's OK to enjoy life—so get into this pool and start,' he called to her.

Every second of Michelle's upbringing had been geared towards following orders. But this one sent a thrill through her.

Throwing off her dressing gown, she dived straight into the water. Once beneath its surface, the simple feeling of freedom relaxed her in a rush. The chill shock invigorated her, as Alessandro had promised. She surfaced, laughing and splashing. Looking around to orientate herself, she saw his dark head dip beneath the water again. Suddenly she felt his hands on her legs. Frictionless, they glided upwards over her body. Flipping onto her back, Michelle kicked away towards the side of the pool with frantic strokes. When she reached it, gasping, he was right beside her.

'No—please don't fool about, Alessandro. I'm not a very good swimmer!'

He smiled, his white teeth as perfect as his reply. 'That dive looked pretty impressive to me.'

Michelle giggled. 'It gets the shock over quickly. I'd rather do that than suffer inch by inch, edging down the steps.'

As she spoke, he looked down at her legs through the shimmering water. She blushed.

'You're an athlete.' He nodded at the pale marks exposed by her bikini. 'I can tell from your *bronzage*.'

During her few precious weeks of freedom Michelle had heard plenty of French spoken with a local accent. She had heard it spoken with an English accent, too. But this was the first time she had heard it given an Italian glow. She couldn't help laughing at the sound.

'No, I'm not! I just run whenever I get the time. It helps me think through my problems.'

'I'm amazed a pretty young woman like you has any problems. The immaculate state of the villa shows how good you are at your job. What else is there to worry about?'

'My mother died in April.'

His expression softened. 'I'm sorry.'

Michelle mentally kicked herself for troubling a guest with her affairs, and spoke quickly to defuse the situation. 'There's no need to apologise. We were never exactly close.'

'Close?' Alessandro's face compressed. He looked down at the fingers of his left hand as they spread out beneath the water. 'Some relationships are a waste of good working time. My own mother couldn't have picked me out of a police line-up.'

Michelle was so stunned she forgot to be polite. 'You can't mean that?'

He gazed across the water to the villa's herb garden. She guessed it wasn't because he was admiring the ornamental thyme.

'Everything I've achieved in my life has been in spite of my family, not because of them.'

Michelle wondered if his remark had anything to do

with those sacked relatives. She decided it was better not to ask.

'Then I'm sorry for you. Even *my* mother wasn't as bad as that.'

His attention snapped straight back to her. 'Don't waste your sympathy on me. It will only lead to trouble.'

Curious, she put her head on one side. 'What do you mean?'

His eyes were twin pools of mystery. 'If you keep looking at me like that, Michelle, you'll soon find out.'

Chilly rivulets of water trickled from her hair and she shivered. The points of her nipples were rising—and not only from the cold. It was the way Alessandro's gaze was totally focussed on her eyes. She could almost feel him searching her soul. No one had ever studied her so intently—not in her whole life. If she was honest, no one had paid any attention to her at all. They only noticed when she *hadn't* done something. The interview she'd missed because her mother had destroyed her portfolio, the single occasion she had been too sick to turn out for Spicer and Co…

'You have a fascinating face, Michelle. Let me draw you,' he said abruptly.

In all her years of sketching Michelle had never had the nerve to ask a stranger to pose for her. She thought of all those lost opportunities and wished she could be spontaneous, like Alessandro. He had come straight out with a suggestion she would never have been brave enough to make in a million years. So many times she had felt the urge to sketch or paint a person, but had been too shy to do anything about it. Now he was showing her how it should be done.

'I—I don't know.' She scraped her wet hair back from her face to give herself time to think. 'I work for Mr Bartlett, really, and if he found out I was lounging around being drawn, when I should be busy in the house…'

Alessandro threw off her objection. 'You're working for me at the moment. Not Terence.'

Michelle paused. There was nothing she could say except, 'If you put it like that, I can't refuse.'

He smiled. 'Yes…' he said thoughtfully. 'The more I see of you, Michelle, the more I realise you're wasted here. You ought to be immortalised somehow. And I'm exactly the man to do it. Wait here. I'll go and fetch my things.'

She had no choice. He vaulted out of the pool and picked up a robe from one of the poolside chairs. He pulled it on and walked quickly into the villa.

Michelle knew she should be feeling cold. She wasn't. The sight of his muscles sleek with water had brought a slow-burning fire to life deep within her body. Alessandro Castiglione had a lot to answer for. From the moment he'd landed he had invaded every part of her life. First he'd stopped her sleeping. Then he'd aroused her by touch, outside the studio house. Now he had persuaded her to wait for him, wet through and waist-deep in water.

As he disappeared from sight, a chill wind rippled across the pool. Michelle's skin contracted with the cold. Sinking beneath the wavelets, she let the water waft her feet off the floor of the pool. She knew she ought to thrash through a few lengths to warm herself up. Her heart wasn't in it. Exercise no longer had the power to distract her. All she could think of was

Alessandro. Big, strong Alessandro Castiglione. He acted the part of blasé tycoon to perfection, but his bitter-chocolate eyes told a different story. When Michelle shivered now, it was at the thought of his deep brown gaze. If only she could decode its meaning.

Twisting in the water, she saw Alessandro walking back towards the pool. He was dressed now in jeans and a tight white tee shirt. His muscles were still on display, and Michelle felt them through her fantasies. Those jeans were so well cut they were obviously made for him. 'Casual' still meant 'designer chic' in his circles. The sketchbook under his arm was bound in leather, and he was carrying a long metal container. He put this down beside one of the poolside chairs.

'If you could swim a few lengths for me, Michelle, I'll try out a few ideas…I need something to make my working days worthwhile. Art is my therapy.'

'And mine. I always wanted to go to art college, but it wasn't possible for me to finish the course,' Michelle said shyly.

He was already rifling through the contents of his art box. Selecting a piece of willow charcoal, he made a few swift, sweeping strokes across his sketchbook.

'A little taster for you.' He showed her the pad. She was amazed. In a few strokes he had laid her down on his plain white sheet with nothing more than a sliver of burnt wood.

'You swim slowly, up and down.'

As he sketched, he asked her all sorts of questions about her own work. His conversation was light and insubstantial—until he asked her something that really burst her bubble.

'What made you give up your art course?'

She didn't answer for a while. Then she rolled onto her back to watch him.

'The answer to that is the same as it is to most of your other questions—my mother,' she said at last. 'Mum didn't consider art to be a proper job. There was no room for anything in my life unless she thought it had value. As a child, I was a disappointment to her. If I couldn't be beautiful, then I had to be useful.'

Alessandro frowned. Michelle was struggling to keep her mind on their conversation, but his disapproving expression helped keep her on track.

'"Art isn't a job, it's almost as much a waste of time as reading."' She quoted one of her mother's favourite sayings.

Alessandro's mood darkened further. 'I thought you said in the studio house that you had some books?'

'I do—and that was the problem. They're art books, and Mum hated them most of all. If I wasn't painting or drawing then I was reading about it. She thought I was doing it to spite her.'

This softened his expression, but only a fraction. 'It might be for the best. I'm in the trade, and art colleges turn out far too many indifferent graduates, in my opinion.'

Alessandro worked quickly, changing medium and trying out several grades of paper. He was enjoying this. Any man could take a woman—Alessandro did, frequently—but this was something altogether different. The more he worked on his sketches of her, the more relaxed he became and his stress fell away. It was a circle of satisfaction.

Eventually he put down his work and stretched, long and luxuriously. The sun felt good.

'Shall I stop swimming?' Michelle called as he stood watching her, hands on his hips.

'Yes. Come and lie on one of these loungers for a while.'

The water accepted her once again, showering her with a thousand droplets at she swam towards the steps. Alessandro watched them tumbling over her smooth wet skin. Each time she raised her arm he marvelled at the perfect curve, the sleek, easy beauty of her. Stepping out onto the hot white tiles, she slicked her wet hair back from her face. He felt his body rise in anticipation.

Grabbing a towel, he enveloped her in its folds. Michelle immediately pulled up a corner and made to rub at her hair.

'Wait—leave that. I want you to look as though you've just left the water. Relaxed, and soaking up the sun.' He took her hand to lead her over to the seats.

In a flash Michelle was swept right back to his goodnight kiss. Alessandro took away her towel and, dropping it in a heap, told her to sit down on the sun lounger.

'Do you want me to do anything special?'

'You look just fine as you are.' His gaze grazed her body appreciatively. 'All you need to do is lie back and close your eyes.'

It took Michelle a little while to get comfortable, and longer to relax.

'I feel a bit self-conscious,' she said apprehensively. She often wore a bikini, but this was the first time she had been within touching distance of a man as gorgeous as Alessandro.

'Don't worry. I've drawn dozens of women—most of them wearing less than you are now.'

Michelle giggled. That made her feel so much more comfortable in his company. But still, when his hand reached out to arrange her wet hair, she flinched.

'Did I hurt you, Michelle?'

'No—not at all. I just have this thing about being touched, that's all. I *know* I'm never going to be struck again, but my body isn't so sure.'

She tried to laugh it off, but Alessandro was shocked. He withdrew a fraction, until her smile reassured him.

'Then I shall be very careful how I position you,' he smiled.

He was more than careful. Each time he reached out to touch her, he hesitated before making contact. She had the double pleasure of anticipation and effect. His touch when it came was so light it was evocative of their evening in the starlight. She could hardly bear it. She knew exactly how each touch would feel, because she had already imagined the grain of his fingertips drifting across her skin. When she reacted with goose pimples, it wasn't from any chill.

Alert as ever, Alessandro fastened his attention on a droplet of water coursing over the downy skin of her forearm.

'Tell me if you get too cold,' he murmured, reaching for the towel. With one long, slow movement, he stroked down the entire length of her arm.

As his touch trailed away, she sighed. It was a sound of total contentment. She leaned back against a cushion and closed her eyes.

'Before you settle down, I think I'll have your hair

over *this* shoulder…' He swept her wet hair around and settled it, lock by lock.

Feeling his fingers stroking each strand into place sent shimmers of energy through Michelle's body. Alessandro had started wiping droplets from her skin and she shivered. As a trickle of water meandered over the generous curve of her breast his fingertips reached out to trace it…

CHAPTER FOUR

A LITTLE cry of anticipation escaped from her lips.

He stopped. His hand was hovering so close to her skin she could feel its warmth. It raised her temperature faster than the sun.

'I can see you're getting cold.' He leaned back, letting his hand fall onto his thigh with a slap. 'Come on, let's get inside—I've made you suffer long enough.' His rich accent rolled over one fantasy, but with smooth assurance he replaced it with another. 'I've arranged a little treat to thank you for your patience.'

'Oh, but you shouldn't have,' Michelle stammered, secretly feeling very glad that he had.

Waving aside her pleasantries, Alessandro picked up two more big towels from the neatly folded pile on the poolside chair next to his. Swirling one around her shoulders, he draped a second over her wet hair. Michelle revelled in their soft, sun-warmed folds. That was luxurious enough. Then she felt his hands moving over them, blotting moisture from her shoulders and hair. She leaned into his touch, enjoying more intimacy than she had ever imagined.

'This is more than a treat, it's heavenly!' she murmured.

'*Dio*—this isn't it.' He chuckled. 'There will be warm croissants and hot chocolate for your breakfast. That's the surprise. I'm guessing you won't have eaten yet?'

Michelle shook her head. She hoped nerves wouldn't stop her eating now! To be served by a guest would be a real turnaround.

He was already heading for the villa. She followed him at a respectful distance, but the gulf between them couldn't stop her dreaming. The villa Jolie Fleur was her workplace. This morning she was almost entering it as a guest. Her normally quick footsteps slowed, and she paused on the threshold. It was a beautiful house, ten times the size of the poky flat she had left behind in England. Pastel paint and mirrors were everywhere. She tried to concentrate on the flower arrangements. This was a great opportunity to see the place through the eyes of a visitor, and she was glad to discover it looked really good.

Alessandro had complimented her on her housekeeping, and that meant a lot. Now he had arranged breakfast. She had never been given a meal by anyone she worked for. It was unlikely to happen again, and definitely not with anyone as gorgeous as Alessandro Castiglione! Michelle was determined to enjoy every second, and make the experience last as long as possible.

'What are you waiting for?' he called back at her over his shoulder. Then he walked on. The crooked smile he flashed so rarely had hidden depths. It made her yearn for his full attention, but it wasn't to be.

'Fancy me having my breakfast served by the world's most eligible bachelor!' she breathed as he led her into the enormous kitchen.

'That's just a title from the tabloids. The woman hasn't been born who can tie me down.' He smiled wolfishly as he directed her out onto the sun-drenched terrace. 'This is to thank you for acting as my model.'

The terrace's stunning sea view was framed by pink bougainvillaea. It made the perfect setting for breakfast. When Michelle had thawed out over a mug of hot chocolate they ate warm buttery croissants, brioches and apricot conserve. She was so nervous she spent more time pretending to admire the view than she did eating. That way she could watch Alessandro.

He ate well, and didn't have much patience with her excuses of not being hungry. With his encouragement, she eventually ate almost as much as he did. Later, over a cup of creamy cappuccino, she relaxed back in her chair and tried to decide whether the sea or the sky was the lovelier shade of blue.

'I could stay here all day,' she said eventually.

'*Perché no*? Why don't you?'

'Because I have to work, of course.'

Alessandro looked around the spotless terrace, and beyond it into the gleaming kitchen. Finally his gaze turned on her.

'This place looks tidy enough to me.'

Reaching out, he brushed a pastry crumb from the sleeve of her robe. It was such an intimate gesture Michelle tensed, wondering how he would follow it up. All he did was look at her, long and intently. It was the same expression he'd used when trying to capture her in his sketchbook.

'It won't take me long to settle into the studio house. Then I shall be able to start planning my next painting properly. I hope you're prepared for me to haunt you day and night, until I get all your features exactly right?'

If only you knew how you haunt me already, Michelle thought. *You are the cause of my sleepless nights*. A delicious tension increased inside her each time she looked into those melting brown eyes.

He checked his watch, and the moment evaporated. 'What time does the caretaker arrive?'

Instantly Michelle knew he had moved on. It signalled the end of her fantasy. He was dismissing her. Much as she wanted to stay, Michelle knew it was for the best. If the caretaker arrived to see her leaving the villa in her dressing gown, she would never hear the end of it.

With a sigh, she realised she couldn't spin out her time languishing in the villa any longer. This was his holiday. But it wasn't hers. She took as long as possible packing up the breakfast things and loading the dishwasher, just to be near him. But however long she lingered, the evil moment couldn't be put off for ever. Eventually she had to say it.

'Thank you so much for breakfast, Alessandro. Now I really must go.'

'Goodbye, Michelle.'

She left the house feeling flat and disappointed. He had changed in an instant, almost as though he'd sensed she might be getting ideas about him. His manner at the pool had been so relaxed and charming. It had put all sorts of crazy ideas in her head. Now he seemed to be doing his best to put up a barrier of indifference. She couldn't help wondering why—and dreaming about what she might do about it.

* * *

Alessandro was restless for the entire day. He couldn't settle to anything. The morning newspaper didn't tell him anything he hadn't already heard from his business associates. Opening the book Michelle had lent him released a drift of her perfume. His eyes tracked across the page, but somehow the words didn't sink in. Instead of Renaissance art he kept being distracted by modern beauty.

Michelle moved around the villa almost silently, freshening flower arrangements, topping up drinks trays, plumping cushions. She never made the first move, but whenever he spoke to her she would pause and talk shyly with him—whether it was about Raphael, the day's menus or something as mundane as the weather.

He took lunch in the garden that day, but that didn't help either. Michelle had moved outside too, gathering lavender from the herb garden. He couldn't see her from his seat on the terrace, but the sound of snipping scissors and the fragrance of crushed flowers told him exactly what she was doing. It reminded him of their evening talk, with all those warm, intimate scents and sounds. He could visualise it so perfectly he began sketching her from memory.

The women in his circle rarely showed the natural beauty and honesty of Michelle. She was unique. His own mother had been a shop girl, until Old Sandro Castiglione had tried hauling her up the social ladder. She had loved the lifestyle but hated the life. All the Castiglione men had lived to regret being related to her. Alessandro grimaced at the memory. Now his world was full of women who rattled on about clothes and make-up as though it should mean something. They were a complete mystery to him.

Early on in his adult life, he discovered that the more money you gave women, the noisier their demands became. There had been one woman who had taken all he had to offer, and more. Then, when he'd least expected it, she had delivered a blow that had almost destroyed him. She had used him as a pawn to make her husband jealous. Experience was a harsh teacher. These days Alessandro took care to keep moving. He took control. It was the only way to enjoy life.

He spent the rest of that day working on the sketches he had made of Michelle. That made his sense of dissatisfaction worse. She claimed she didn't mind him distracting her, to check the exact line of her shoulders or the precise size of her eyes. Each time he promised it would be the last. He admired the way she pretended to be disappointed, with an almost professional skill.

As the day dwindled away he shut himself in the studio house, determined to get down to work. After all, the place was perfect. The light was good; there were no distractions; he could lay all his artist's materials out. The only thing it lacked was a live model. He wondered about going to check on the original for a fifth and final time, but he could hardly disturb her again. There were limits—even for him.

He roamed over to the French doors, which were standing open. Shadows were lengthening out in the garden. A walk through that oasis of calm might help him to cool down. Throwing his sketchbook aside for the final time, he strode out into the evening.

He spotted Michelle almost at once, and stopped before she saw him. She was standing on the grass, only a hundred yards from the studio house, gazing along the flower-filled border. A playful breeze pressed the thin cotton of her uniform against her body. The gentle curve of her breasts contrasted beautifully with her small, well-defined waist. He noticed all this with an artist's eye, but testosterone filled in plenty more details. Beneath that dress her spine curved into the flare of her bottom—which would be soft and peach-like, he knew. And he had already seen those long, slender legs in the pool that morning.

Arousal drew him on. When she turned and saw him, her lips parted as though she was about to speak.

No words were needed. His hands reached out for her as he approached, and he drew her into his arms.

Shock was almost as powerful a feeling as lust, Michelle realised. She tried to speak, but once she felt the insistence of his flesh against hers she was lost. Her body trembled, and she gasped at the power of its response. Then Alessandro eclipsed the setting sun as he kissed her with a passion so primitive all her inhibitions were swept away. She returned his kiss, her heart beating erratically as she revelled in the experience. She was being tasted by the man who filled her days and dreams.

Clutching at him as though she would never let him go, she raked his back with her fingers. He responded by moulding her body beneath his hands. She was his. Dizzy with a tumble of emotions, Michelle knew she was unleashing feelings she could never control. Her body pounded with an urgent burning desire, flooding through her veins in a tidal surge.

She had never felt like this before. Her body reacted purely on instinct, alive to all the sensations he was igniting in her. His kisses released her mouth and she threw back her head with a moan. Alessandro's mouth skimmed over the sensitised skin of her throat. Time lost all meaning as her torment increased. Her body sang with an almost unbearable torment. A heavy drawing feeling deep within her made Michelle press herself against his unyielding body. She leaned into his touch, feeling the most feminine parts of her opening, waiting for his touch.

Alessandro was more than ready for the experience. He pulled her close, the ridge of his erection rubbing against her. With a gurgle of pleasure she let her hands swim from his shoulders to his waist, then on. Light-headed with longing, she caressed the taut curve of his buttocks—but her fingers craved more. Soon they were dancing over his groin, desperate to discover its mystery.

'Oh, Alessandro…' she breathed.

If he didn't want her heart, then she was ready to give him the only thing she knew he would accept. As his hands caressed the heavy fullness of her breasts, she struggled to release his zip. His kisses closed over her mouth again as she shut her eyes and pushed her hand inside his jeans. With a lurch of excitement she discovered he was naked inside them. In mounting wonder she ran her fingers over the rigid length of him.

'*No*—not yet.'

She reacted with pained surprise at the note of command in his voice. He moved back a fraction—far enough to unfasten her uniform. He removed it from her body in one practised movement. She gasped, but he wasn't finished yet. Pulling down her bra straps, he peeled back the lace and put his mouth to her naked breast. While his hands cradled and caressed their fullness, his teeth teased first one nipple and then the other into hard beads.

Michelle was faint with pleasure. Her breath came in ragged gasps as she called his name into the lonely dusk. She clutched at him, and their bodies became one.

Revelling in sensations they both needed to satisfy, Alessandro laid her down gently on the camomile lawn. It was warm and fragrant, reflecting the primitive heat of their passion. With a pang Alessandro wondered if his need for her was simply a symptom of his shallow lifestyle. If crossing the divide between his world and hers just introduced a little danger into the relentless routine of his life. A million thoughts formed and vanished in his mind as Michelle moved beneath his body. She had a supple delight he needed to experience.

Rolling over the sweet herbs, he took possession of her. All his consciousness was centred on filling the void inside himself. He thrust into her, feeling resistance and hearing her little cry as her muscles tensed and then closed around him. She made a sound of the deepest, darkest female pleasure, arching her back to meet him until they melded into one being. He leaned forward, entering her as deeply as he had done in his dreams. His pleasure was so intense he wondered how he had managed to resist her for so long.

Michelle clung to him, riding the waves of new sensation and wishing it would never come to an end. She wanted to absorb all his body, to give herself to him as completely as he was possessing her.

This was her life, and she was giving it to him. Nothing would ever compare to this moment, here with Alessandro, beneath the darkening Mediterranean sky.

'Oh, Alessandro,' she whispered, as soon as the breath seeped back into her lungs. 'I never dreamed making love could be as wonderful as that. I wanted my first time to be the best…'

Her lids were heavy with emotion and her words full of sincerity, but they froze Alessandro to the bone.

What the hell have I done? he thought, knowing full well it was the worst possible thing. Gently, but as quickly as he could without hurting her, he withdrew. The little gasp she gave told him more than he wanted to know.

'*Dio*, Michelle. I'm sorry…'

'Don't be. It was fantastic.' She reached up, cupping his face with her hand. Her eyes were liquid with sincerity.

Alessandro was appalled. How could he have been so stupid? He had heard that tone, seen that expression and felt that touch in his dim and distant past. It had spelled disaster then, and would do again.

'It was a mistake,' he said firmly, hardening his heart and looking away in case she winced. 'It should never have happened.'

'I know. I *know*,' she said quickly, in a small voice that seemed to come from far away.

He felt her moving beside him. Unable to look her in the face, he rolled towards her again, pulling her head into his shoulder and holding her close. Everything had changed between them. He had expected tears and accusations. Instead he'd got silence. That was worse. He had hurt her, and not only physically. The knowledge pierced him like a blade. It was the first time someone else's pain had rebounded on him, and it was a shock. Facts and figures were so much easier to control than feelings—especially when they belonged to other people.

It made him think. This would be another sleepless night for him, he vowed, but it would be one with a purpose.

He had work to do.

CHAPTER FIVE

Four months later

ALESSANDRO sat alone in the boardroom of the House of Castiglione. He looked over the accounts he had been handed a second and then a third time. The figures refused to make sense.

His people kept telling him what a success Michelle was making of her new life back in England, but he couldn't see it. When he looked at the dust-dry columns of figures all he saw was her luscious body, so soft and willing beneath his hands.

His initial anger over his own irresponsibility had taken a while to subside. When he had arranged for his charitable trust to set her up in business, he'd assumed that would be an end to it. His growing hunger to experience her again disturbed him. The mere sight of her name on this file inflamed his need. Something had to be done to get her out of his head—once and for all. He wanted to possess her again, to take her with the same fierce passion that had overwhelmed her on that sultry Mediterranean night. Nothing less would satisfy him.

Throwing the papers aside, he gave orders that he was leaving for England—right away.

Melting with anticipation, Michelle held her breath. Alessandro's smiling eyes looked into hers as though she was the only woman in the world—now and for ever. They were lying on soft, sweet, herb-scented grass in a pool of shade. Above them, leaves rustled in a hot, dry breeze. His hand traced the flickering pattern of shadows over her nakedness. As his fingers trailed from her shoulder, around the curve of her spine to the plump softness of her hips, she moaned and drew closer to the security of his body. He was about to place a tender kiss on her lips—

The alarm clock catapulted Michelle out of her dreams, straight back into real life.

For a long time she refused to open her eyes. She knew millions of people would kill for the chance of the life she had now. That didn't make waking up any easier. Alessandro had written himself out of her life. Oh, he had been madly generous, arranging for his people to set her up with her own art gallery and the Cotswold cottage she had always dreamed of owning. But his guilt had come at a terrible price.

Michelle was still only gradually coming to accept that she would never see him again. The only time memories could bring her pleasure was while she slept. Her dreams always focussed on the irresistible, adorable Alessandro, not on his heartless reality. Once she woke, the pain of their parting was too much to bear.

Waking destroyed the only pleasure she had left in life. This wasn't the sun-soaked South of France. It was England at the dreariest time of year. The only fragrance in her life now came from the lavender bags she had brought back with her. She groaned. It couldn't be morning already, could it? Squinting at her alarm clock, she tried to make out its digital display. Before she could manage it, the realisation of what mornings had come to mean hit her like a lead weight.

She rolled over, pulling the duvet over her head. *Please, please let me have just five more minutes' calm before the heaving storm begins—*

It was no good. Her stomach was already turning somersaults. *How can one tiny baby wreak such havoc?* she thought, staggering into the bathroom to lean her forehead against the cold china of the washbasin. She shut her eyes.

If only events could be blacked out so easily. She had given her heart to a man with a terrible reputation, who had dropped plenty of hints about his hatred of commitment. The one time she had tried to contact him directly his firewall of personal staff had closed ranks around him. She had been abandoned, and it was no more than she should have expected from a man like Alessandro Castiglione. What hope was there for someone as stupid as she was?

When she began to feel better, she opened her eyes. There was no point in raking over past mistakes, but she couldn't help it. Gently she stroked the front of her nightdress. Her life must centre on what was best for her baby now. Memories of its father were all she had left— and one single letter.

A chill ran over her body. Suddenly she was back in the villa Jolie Fleur, the morning after their lovemaking. How she had tortured herself as she'd got ready for her working day, wondering how she could ever look Alessandro in the eyes again. And then she had opened the door of his suite and found her book on Raphael, returned with a note to say that business had called him away but that his staff would be in touch with her.

Only the abandoned house had heard her tears. Right from the start she had known he was lying. How could work have contacted him when she knew his phone wasn't working? Running straight to the studio house, she had found it empty and abandoned. Alessandro had taken all his art equipment and was gone.

When two smartly dressed representatives of the Castiglione Foundation had arrived later in the week to present her with the keys to a house and a business in the most exclusive part of the English countryside, Michelle's impulse had been to throw it straight back in their faces. But although she was proud, she wasn't stupid. She had listened to their assurances that Signor Castiglione often used his wealth to set hard-working, deserving people up in business. They'd known all about her temporary contract coming to an end, and that she would soon need a new job. It had seemed like the ideal solution to all her problems. Like winning Alessandro's heart, security had been an impossible dream for Michelle. Accepting his offer would satisfy them both.

After completing her contract at the villa, she had returned to a new life in her old country with everything she had ever dreamed about—and more. Within weeks she had discovered she was pregnant. It was both the best and the worst thing that could have happened. With another life to protect, Michelle couldn't afford to grieve for what she had lost. Instead she had a whole new set of worries.

How could she give her baby a better childhood than her own if it was going to grow up without a father?

Michelle always arrived at the gallery very early to make sure everything was spotless. This village was a tourist honeypot in the Cotswolds, famous for its royal connections. Her clients loved Michelle's efficiency, and she never disappointed them.

She went in through the front door, half noticing a sleek, pale blue car prowling around the market square. Checking her mobile, she disappeared into the office. The phone had been bought during her very first days of freedom, straight after her mother's death. It had been an important milestone on Michelle's road to a whole new life.

I've certainly accelerated along it since then, she reflected as the bell on the shop door announced she had forgotten to lock the door behind her.

'I'm afraid we aren't open yet, but please look around!' she called out, in her best gallery-owner's voice.

Concentrating on her phone, she pressed the button to retrieve her messages. As usual, the only messages were from friends and customers. Another twenty-four hours had passed without any word from Alessandro. That made two thousand, nine hundred and twenty-eight hours in total so far. Not that she was counting, of course. There was no point. He'd always stressed he wasn't interested in commitment. And since returning to England, she had found out exactly how true that was.

She addressed every bit of correspondence about her

business direct to him, but the Castiglione Foundation's faceless finance department always dealt with it. Not once had Alessandro ever got in touch himself. Every single magazine she'd ever read warned that holiday romances like hers always led to disaster. *So why didn't I believe them?* she thought bitterly. *It would have saved me an ocean of tears.*

'Michelle?'

His voice swept in from the gallery, rich with all the bitter darkness of continental chocolate. It was unmistakeable. She froze, struggling to believe what she had heard.

'Alessandro?' she whispered. Then common sense stopped her rushing out into the gallery. She wasn't going to make a fool of herself a second time. She had shrugged on a shroud of cynicism the day Alessandro had abandoned her at the villa. It was time to see how well it fitted. She needed answers, and she turned to confront him.

Time stood still. All her rage and disappointment went into suspended animation. She stared up at him, transfixed. His tall, imposing figure instantly filled her mind and her senses with a heady mix of memories. Every important detail, from his luxuriant dark hair and piercing graphite eyes to the tang of his individual after-shave and all that essential maleness, was exactly as she remembered. Today he wore a classically tailored suit. A tie in midnight-blue silk and solid gold cufflinks graced his formal white shirt. The effect was understated, and obviously expensive. He was standing before her in the totally desirable flesh, and it made quite a contrast to the naked splendour Michelle was trying her hardest not to remember. She knew the only thing that should matter to her was why he had walked out on her, all those lonely weeks ago.

But as she met his gaze Michelle forgot everything but the torrid passion he fired in her. It sizzled through her veins, drawing her close enough to inhale the distinctive warm scent of his aftershave. It made her want him. She had been forced to put on armour when he abandoned her, just to get through every day. Now he was here she wanted him to remove it, piece by piece— but her body had other ideas.

A second, different sort of surge made her step back, both hands reaching for her throat in a mixture of panic and embarrassment.

'Oh… Oh, dear… I feel sick…'

'I don't normally have this effect, *tesoro*—' Alessandro began, but his smile vanished as she shook her head.

'No, I mean *really* sick—'

He sidestepped smartly as she rushed past him and into the tiny bathroom beyond the office. She reached it just in time. Almost immediately she felt Alessandro at her side. When she'd finally stopped throwing up, he pushed a wet cloth into her hands. Michelle had never felt so grateful for anything in her life. She pressed it against her face, glad to hide her burning cheeks.

'Is there anything I can do?' he asked, his beautiful accent thick with concern. It broke her heart all over again.

'You've done enough already, don't you think?' she croaked.

Taking the flannel from her hot, clammy hands, he replaced it with a glass of ice-cold water. When she had finished drinking, he took it back. Then he helped her to her feet. Feeling as weak as a kitten, Michelle clung to him. For a few seconds she deluded herself she was back in heaven. Then she discovered she wasn't the only one who had changed. Alessandro was not melting against her as he had done on their glorious first and last coupling. His body was tense and unyielding. He reached for her hands, held them for a moment, and then released himself.

The ice in his voice matched his wintry expression. 'I've set you up with a home and a job for life. You didn't have either when we met.'

There was a dangerous look in his eyes that made her wonder what more could go wrong with her life. When she challenged him, she soon found out. Her dreams met reality and came off worse.

'You want me to be grateful? For the fact you've been keeping me safely at a distance? Is it because you want to feel you've done your duty? Or so I can't embarrass you in front of your friends, like Terence Bartlett?' She put all her pain into the words. Her heart had taken a thousand knocks over the past few months, but she had never felt as bad as she did right now. 'You've left me quite literally holding the baby, and you expect me to be *grateful*?'

'No, but if you can't be thankful you could at least—' He stopped and stared. His eyes had been riveted on hers. Now their penetrating gaze dropped slowly, inch by inch, down her face to her body.

Michelle watched the broad expanse of his shoulders rising and falling rapidly. Their irregular rhythm betrayed a seething tumult within him. When he could bring himself to speak, Alessandro had to make an obvious attempt to remain civil.

'You are pregnant? Now, why doesn't that surprise me?' he hissed through the mockery of a grin. 'Children are such good bargaining tools. I hardly need ask if you're going to keep it.'

The image he projected was pure Vesuvius. All those terrible rumours about him came back to taunt her.

'I've been left completely alone in the world. I know what it's like to be unwanted.' Michelle edged her bitter words into the simmering silence between them. 'I have to make amends. What else can I do?'

'I think we've both done far too much already.'

For long moments she watched him in terrified silence. At first his head was bowed. Then gradually he raised it, until his words were being spoken to the top left hand corner of the room.

'From now on it's a matter of damage limitation. It can start with the fiction of a happy reunion between us.'

Michelle stared at him. Back in France this man had taken everything she had to give. When he had vanished from her life it had created a void so vast she knew it could never be filled by anyone else. Now he was standing right here in front of her. She had so many questions they tangled in her throat, silencing her. She wanted to reach out and touch him, to recall that painfully short time they'd spent entwined, but his expression reflected her experience. His eyes blazed.

'How have you got the nerve to stand there so calmly, Michelle?'

The bitter reproach in his voice ignited all her protective instincts.

'I'm making the best of the situation. That's all I can do,' she said staunchly, but colour flared into her cheeks.

Her reaction seemed to draw the sting of his anger. His shoulders relaxed a little.

'Yes. Of course.'

Her anguish increased as the fire in his eyes died and was replaced with distaste, as though he was waiting for her to justify herself. Once he had been closer to her than she had been to herself. That sliver of time they had spent together had been the stuff of fairy tales—*and he still is*, she realised. His soft, dark curls might be shorter now, but they were equally impossible to tame. And the cool aristocracy of his cheekbones remained, though he was thinner. Was he working too hard? She ached to know.

Her news was a hammer-blow to him. She could see that. Despite everything he had put her through, she was desperate to stretch out and comfort him. The familiar rasp of his chin against her palm would feel so very good… With an involuntary shake of her head, she gave up on the idea. Alessandro was clean-shaven now. Even that had changed. Everything was different between them—especially the expectation in his eyes. It had become as hard as mahogany.

'Well? Don't you have anything to say for yourself, Michelle?'

She squared up to him. It had taken the two of them to reach this point. However frightening his reputation, he ought to be told a few home truths.

'Like what, exactly?' She tilted her chin, mirroring his determination. Hurting badly, she struck back in the only way she could. 'You betrayed my trust, Alessandro.

What happened to us? Where did you go? From the moment you left me in France, all I've done is work, eat, sleep—and try to forget you.'

'Well, now you and I are going to give the world the happy-ever-after it wants.' His voice crackled, and she saw defiance in his eyes. 'No bad publicity must ever be allowed to harm my company. The headline *"Billionaire left me pregnant, sobs virgin"* will sell a million newspapers. I'm not in the business of giving journalists an easy life. Last year I sued a tabloid to within an inch of bankruptcy for claiming I had an affair with the wife of a business rival. Now they're waiting to catch me out for real. But it isn't going to happen.'

There was no question about it—whatever 'it' might be. Michelle saw cold determination in his eyes. For the first time since meeting him all those weary months ago she felt fear.

Reaching into his jacket, he pulled out his phone. One long, irritable call later, he shut it and confronted her again.

'My people will tip off the media that I am meeting you here today. There will be a photo opportunity, and a press release drafted to go with the pictures,' he told her. 'That will keep the papers happy for a while.'

'Will the handout explain why you haven't been in touch with me since—?'

A raised brow from Alessandro snapped off her question, as though his being reminded of their last moments together was nothing more than an irritation to him. Outwardly calm for a moment, he adjusted his tie. Its sleek blue silk was an ideal complement to his dark handmade suit and brilliant white shirt.

'As I always told you in France, I was looking for relaxation, not commitment.'

His voice was stiff with self-justification. He continued smoothing down his sleeves and checking his cufflinks, but as far as Michelle could see nothing about him needed altering. As always, he looked perfect. But to her, right now, he seemed an empty shell. The man who had beguiled her at the villa Jolie Fleur had vanished. She searched his expression, but the more she saw the less she understood.

'If rescuing you today silences the scandalmongers, Michelle, then this is for the best, too.'

As he spoke, the look in his eyes softened slightly. She took another step towards him.

'Why didn't you ever ring me?' she whispered. Suddenly every second of the good times came back to her in sparkling detail, and it hurt. There could be no hiding the resentment in her voice as she added, 'You abandoned me, Alessandro!'

His lids lowered, giving those beautiful dark eyes an added mystery. 'You have hardly played fair with *me*.'

'I couldn't help it!' she wailed, but Alessandro wasn't listening.

'But I can. And I'm going to.'

He spoke with grim determination, but for a second it was tempered by his expression. He lowered his chin and arched his brows, and in that moment a spark of recognition flared within Michelle. Somewhere beneath this flinty new exterior was the Alessandro of midnight conversation and dawn swimming. Passion had sizzled through Michelle's veins then. It was rekindled now, as she drew close enough to inhale the distinctive warm scent of his aftershave. Her body urgently wanted to make physical contact with his. It might hold the key to her prison of regret. Warmth rushed over her skin as she willed her hand to rise and stroke his cheek, but her body had other ideas.

A second, different sort of surge made her step back, both hands reaching for her throat in a mixture of panic and embarrassment.

'Oh… Oh, dear… I feel sick again…'

'It will be better to get it over with now, before we leave,' he said with resignation. 'We will be safely in Italy by lunchtime.'

Michelle didn't have time to ask what he meant. The word-association between 'lunch' and 'food' sent her stomach over the edge again.

His jaw was resolute as he knelt down beside her a second time. His efficiency with wet cloths and cold drinks in the face of the turmoil going on inside her body made Michelle feel completely hopeless. She groaned, and then groaned a second time as she thought back to his mention of journalists, travel to Italy, and all the on-lookers it was bound to involve.

'Oh, no—what will everyone think?' she moaned.

Alessandro flung his hands high with a ferocious exclamation in Italian. 'At a time like this she worries about *modi*—good manners!' he marvelled, incensed. 'Right now there's only one thing you should be concerned with, *tesoro*—and it isn't other people!'

CHAPTER SIX

IT TOOK her some time to recover. Alessandro made tea, and a lot of calls on his mobile in terse Italian. By the time Michelle felt stable enough to leave the back office and walk into the gallery there were half a dozen photographers gathered outside.

'They're never far away. The Cotswolds are full of royal residences and megastar hideaways to be staked out,' he explained with scorn for the subject.

'And they'd abandon all that for a shot of you?' she said cautiously.

'I can't help that. I never asked to be catapulted into the public eye, but it's something I have to live with. Like you, I must do the best I can. It's really only the House of Castiglione that is important to me.'

She gave a wry smile, unable to deny it. His work *was* seemingly the only thing he cared about. Alessandro had stressed there would be no future for them. But at the time it hadn't stopped her fantasising about living the simple life of an artist's wife. Now her dreams past and present burned to ashes under the searing gaze of the world's press.

I knew my holiday romance was too good to be true, she thought sadly to herself.

'Well, I suppose I should be grateful for your help. I could have done without your army of fans, though.' She almost managed to smile, but when Alessandro tried to do the same it ended with a shake of his head.

'As I said, I have a rescue plan, Michelle. I'm offering you an escape, should you wish to take it.'

He bit through his words like silver foil. Whatever he was offering, Michelle could see it involved him in great sacrifice. She thought back to what she had given him that glorious Mediterranean evening.

When she spoke, her voice was dangerously quiet. 'You abandoned me, Alessandro.'

'Now you know why.' He gestured towards the long lenses trained on her, ready to snap the moment they stepped out of the gallery door. The firm line of his jaw still had the power to make her feel weak at the knees, but now it was clenched with barely concealed anger.

All the hours of waiting, the worry and the fear rose up and forced her to challenge his shark-sleek fury.

No, I don't! I don't know anything, Alessandro! she thought. *I don't know why you left the villa so fast, I don't know why my business is being besieged by paparazzi at eight o'clock in the morning, and worst of all—* She tried to fight back tears of confusion. He had been a wonderful man of mystery during his time at the villa Jolie Fleur, but that same blank canvas was now a frightening, frustrating shield raised against her.

Looking up at him, she whispered, 'What happened to the funny, romantic artist I met in France?'

'Life. That's what happened to him,' he said briskly.

'It's what goes on behind the scenes when you're busy having a good time. Now, give me the key to your house. Your things will need to be packed.'

Dizzy with exhaustion, and hardly able to think straight, Michelle nearly laughed out loud. 'Wait! Wind back a bit—you're going too fast! How am I supposed to get back to Rose Cottage through all those photographers? Will they let me past?' More were arriving by the minute. 'I can't face them feeling like this...'

He drew in a long, deep breath. Michelle studied his face, desperate for clues. It was hopeless. His raven eyes were more full of mystery than ever.

'You won't need to. My people will do it all for you. That's how things will be from now on.' He spoke slowly and deliberately, as though she were a child and he was a parent hardly able to keep a lid on his anger.

'Here? Or in Italy?' she said, piecing together the fragments of his earlier announcement.

'At my home, of course. You can't possibly stay here after all this.' He cocked his head in the direction of the crowds outside. 'I don't intend to leave you and my child here a moment longer. Left here alone, you're a danger to yourself. And to my business,' he finished bitterly.

'Is it true that you sacked your own relatives from the House of Castiglione?' She couldn't stop herself asking the awful question.

'I really didn't expect that *you* would listen to gossip.' His voice was a diamond tip, etching the remains of her heart. 'I thought you were above that sort of thing, Michelle. But at least it shatters the last illusion either of us might have. We know nothing about each other, so we can start our new life together from scratch.'

'Our new life?' She stared at him, bemused.

'That's what I said. Now, let's go. The paparazzi will sit around outside for days, waiting for what they want. They have endless patience. I don't.' He looked her over with a critical eye. 'Do you have your keys?'

'Yes.'

'Show me.'

Distracted by the arrival of a huge man in shades and a sharp suit outside the front door of the gallery, Michelle rummaged in her handbag. She found nothing. As Alessandro fidgeted, she went through each of her pockets in turn. With relief she put her hand on them in the last possible place they could have been hiding, and pulled them out with a flourish.

'At last. Now, we go.' He nodded, ushering her towards the door. 'Leave me to field any questions.' His accent was thickened with tension.

The giant was obviously employed by Alessandro. He opened the gallery door to let them out. Without a word, Alessandro handed him the key to Rose Cottage. Michelle quailed, until Alessandro's hand fell heavily on her shoulder. 'That's Max. He'll see to your packing. I have a car waiting for us—stay close to me and say nothing.'

She nodded dumbly, and then noticed the beautiful pale blue car she had seen earlier. It was drawn up in the nearest possible parking space, only a few yards away.

'Is that our transport to the airport?'

Alessandro nodded.

'When does our plane leave?'

'It's my own jet, so departure time is the moment we get there. And now—*silencio, per favore.*' He took her arm with cold determination. 'We must smile for the cameras, Michelle.'

She did as she was told.

The crowd surged forward with a sparkle of flash-guns. Far from bundling her through them, as she'd expected, Alessandro stopped and raised his hand.

'Please, ladies and gentlemen! Remember our agreement. Michelle and I will give you the one shot I promised you could have. Then you leave us in peace, OK?'

Michelle wasn't aware what the crowd made of this, because in the same instant Alessandro hijacked all her senses at once. Pulling her into his arms, he kissed her with such verve the universe exploded around them. His mouth pressed hard against hers until all she could think of was the one burst of totally priceless passion they had shared.

Her hands reached up, desperate for the reassurance of his powerful bulk. The fragrance of him, the hard, perfectly defined muscles beneath the designer clothes, brought all her feelings for him powering back. Only one thing was missing. That moment in the garden, when he had reached out to her, his eyes had been alive. Right now they were magnetite, cold and hard, despite the hot fluidity of his body against hers. His fingers dug into her shoulders, but it was a grip of possession, not warmth.

Seething against this conflict of emotions, she held on to him, desperate for encouragement. Instead he drew back, just far enough for his whisper to be heard by Michelle alone.

'There. That's it.' His words to her were deadly as diamonds, but all threat vanished as he turned another winning smile on for the cameras. 'If the photographers among you weren't quick enough to catch it, *peggio per te*! There'll never be another one.'

'You sound awfully sure of that, Alessandro!' Michelle quipped, but his reaction seared her into silence. He shot such a poisonous glare at her that she jumped. It happened so fast no one but Michelle saw it, but it was a look she would never forget.

With an eloquent shrug for the rest of his audience, Alessandro changed his hold on Michelle and started propelling her towards his car. While he might be smiling with those perfect white teeth, all she could focus on was the rigid line of his jaw.

Her shock at his expression turned to horror as questions began firing from every part of the crowd. Alessandro's people had made a good job of alerting the press. More vans were pulling up along Market Street all the time. The forest of satellite aerials grew. This was a worldwide sensation.

Desperate for guidance, she called out to Alessandro. It was a mistake. In the privacy of her office he had been rigid with fury, but the total lack of emotion he turned on her now was far worse. With a smile that did absolutely nothing to soften his features, he turned his cool professionalism on the questioners. They were crowding in on every side. Despite her fear of this new, unrecognisable Alessandro, Michelle found herself shrinking towards his protection. He had a vice-like hold on her hand, and his complexion was pale, but he used every ounce of his easy charm as he spoke to their tormentors.

'Please don't hassle my fiancée, gentlemen.'

As they reached the car, its uniformed chauffeur opened the rear door for her. Michelle was stunned, and stopped. Alessandro let go of her, but his attention never faltered. Sliding his fingers across to the small of her back, he directed her towards the yawning cavern that was the interior. His towering presence blocked her retreat, so there was no chance of bolting back into the familiar sanctuary of her gallery. The driver and the open car door blocked any hope of escape on one side. She cast a hopeless glance in the other direction. Swollen by the arrival of practically all the villagers, the crowd surged forward. If she ran, where could she go?

A ripple of excitement passed through the crowd. Pens clicked, notebooks were flicked.

'Fiancée? But you've never told us about any engagement, Sandro?'

There was a hint of accusation in the anonymous question. The rest of the crowd was quick to echo it. Alessandro laughed it all off.

'For the first time I've surprised you, gentlemen.' He grinned affably, but Michelle saw his mask slip ever so slightly as he added, 'And, please, Sandro was my father's name. I am Alessandro—apart from genetics, my late father and I have absolutely *nothing* in common. OK?'

'Nothing? How about your treatment of pretty girls?' a voice called out.

Alessandro smiled again, but only Michelle was close enough to see that his sudden flush had more to do with rage than flirtation.

'No one who knows me would suggest any such thing,' Alessandro replied lightly, but his eyes were boring holes through Michelle as he did so.

'History looks to be repeating itself, though, doesn't

it? A sudden engagement to an unknown shop girl? Have you got something to hide?' another voice chipped in.

The crowd tasted blood. Excitement bubbled through the whole gathering.

'What do the other members of the House of Castiglione think of all this?' a third interrogator yelled from the back of the gathering.

'No comment,' Alessandro snapped as he guided Michelle forward, her legs almost giving way as she entered the false security of the car's interior.

Even as the door slammed shut behind her the press engulfed the vehicle like a tide. Alessandro dived in from the other side and flicked a switch on the console beside Michelle. Instantly, the car windows became opaque. All the grinning faces outside were reduced to dancing silhouettes as the chauffeur settled himself in the driving seat. Alessandro issued some clipped instructions in Italian. Then he raised an electric partition, effectively sealing the passenger compartment of his car off from the rest of the world.

Michelle fought to control her panic. She had no idea what had been in Alessandro's mind when he'd arrived at her gallery out of the blue, but she knew what the trouble was now. Her news was the cause of all this commotion. Her life had been spinning out of control for weeks. Now Alessandro was throwing it right out of kilter. Things were going from bad to absolutely terrible.

Alessandro secured his seat belt with short, sharp movements. 'Let's get going.'

She needed to scrape together a lot of courage to keep her voice steady in the face of her shattered dreams and his coldly formal fury.

'W-why did you call me your fiancée just then?'

'Because that is what you must be.'

He turned his coal-black eyes on her. They were so lacking in the gentle romance she had once experienced she felt a sudden chill of fear. The words she had once longed to hear were distorted by threat.

'Don't I have any say in the matter, Alessandro?'

He gave a derisory snort. 'You could have been honest with me and said no all those weeks ago. Then none of this would have happened.'

How could he discount the most important moment of her life like that? 'I'm sorry,' she whispered.

'I'm sure you are.' The fingers of his left hand drummed relentlessly on his knee, and he stared out of the window. 'But are you sorry because you wish it had never happened? Or because I've arrived to take control of the situation when you thought you'd be getting everything your own way?'

Michelle couldn't answer. She stared down at her hands, which fractured and blurred as tears filled her eyes. She prayed he wasn't thinking about a termination. It had crossed her mind for a split second, but she knew she could never have taken that route. How could Alessandro, a man who was driven around in a car the size of a super-tanker, ever understand how despair felt?

She shut her eyes and sank back in her seat. She had woken that morning thinking nothing could be worse than a future of loneliness and hard work. Now she knew differently.

Their journey to the airport was tense with silence. Alessandro only spoke to her again when his people had whisked them through the formalities and settled them on his private jet. Alert to his mood, the staff disappeared as fast as they could.

'I assume from that second little exhibition you really *are* carrying my child?'

His voice ran like a switchblade across her nerves. Michelle raised her head, and saw that he must have been winding himself up for a long time to pose the one question that was really preying on his mind. His breathing was irregular, and he nipped his lower lip as he waited for her reply.

'Of course I am. I wouldn't lie to you, Alessandro.'

'In my experience there's no "of course" about it— not where women are concerned.'

His bitterness towards her was one thing. This second-guessing when he hadn't shown any appreciation of her feelings in the past was too much. She was suddenly as cold as he looked.

'How dare you suspect me of lying to you without any proof, Alessandro? Maybe it's the company you keep. I'm sure confidences can be broken and twisted when there's big money on offer. So perhaps I should try and understand how you feel—'

'You never could.' Her appeal was cut off bluntly.

She was aghast. 'Then how can you possibly expect me to marry you if you think that? Surely marriage must be based on understanding?'

He shook his head. 'I *must* marry you. There's no alternative. I won't have a child of mine born illegitimate. Anything less than marriage will give the press exactly the opening they have been waiting for. I've been trying to live down my family's terrible reputation, but the media prefers monsters.

'Last year the papers accused me of having an affair on the basis of nothing more than a few perfectly ordinary photographs taken in a restaurant. I was photographed dining with the wife of a business rival. Knowing my situation, and how much her husband coveted the House of Castiglione, she wanted to buy it for him. We discussed it a few times in secret meetings. I was very tempted, but in the end I decided not to sell. We were photographed during one of our discussions, and the paper made it out as much more. The scandal almost killed her—and their marriage. I sued the rag, and got a retraction of the lies it printed, but the media never forgets something like that. An abandoned woman and a bastard child would give them real ammunition to use against me.'

He looked at her directly, his eyes burning coals of accusation.

'So? Tell me the truth, Michelle. If I hadn't come to fetch you, would you have bothered to tell me about this baby, before you told *them*?'

For one mad moment Michelle had been tempted to keep the whole thing to herself. When she'd got the results of the pregnancy test her impulse had been to run away and hide. And after failed attempts to get in contact with Alessandro she had reconciled herself to being alone with her baby—and her memories. It was the price she would pay for the few days of fantasy life she'd led in France. She had her cottage and her business, but it wouldn't make up for spending the rest of her existence without him and coping alone.

But life didn't get any more real than it was right now. She was pressed into her seat on Alessandro's executive jet like a frightened witness faced with a seasoned prosecuting counsel. Nodding in answer to his question didn't get the reaction she expected. Alessandro exhaled with a noise of disgust.

'So why didn't you tell me straight away?'

Michelle stared out of the window. As the jet gained height her spirits tumbled.

'How could I?' she whispered at last, watching her tears reflected in the glass. They were crossing the coast, and she could have cried an ocean. 'You disappeared, Alessandro! I went straight to the studio house, but it was all locked and shuttered. I waited and waited for you to come back, but you never did. What was I supposed to think when I discovered I was pregnant? That a man who disappeared so fast after the wonderful time we'd shared would be a good father to my baby? I don't think so!'

She turned anguished eyes on her accuser. But he had looked away, his lips set in a determined line. Michelle's frustration erupted in a strangled cry. With only her baby to protect, she had nothing left to lose. However furious Alessandro might be at what she had to say, she no longer cared. He might think he was riding to her rescue, but this wasn't the fairy tale she had dreamed about. She steeled herself to face his rage, but a strange change was working over his features. The muscles in his face relaxed slightly and he moved his head from side to side. Without even really realising it, he'd picked up a coaster and was sketching on it—keeping his hands busy as he thought.

'*Sì…capisco.* But I'm here now.' Instead of shouting her down, his voice was a slow river. It rose around her as he asked, 'Did you ever think about termination?'

She nodded, fighting against the swell of tears that stung her throat and made it so difficult to speak.

'I couldn't bring myself to do it.'

'But you did consider it?'

'It crossed my mind for a second, yes.' Her voice was thin and indistinct.

Scoring a vicious line across his sketch, he turned away, hissing a torrent of Italian at the window beside him. Leaning his elbow against its sill, he pressed the side of his thumb against his mouth.

Please don't say something we'll both regret, she thought hopelessly. Sunlight flooding into the jet's interior cast a halo around him. When he eventually decided how to put his feelings into words, his silhouette became an avenging angel.

'Why didn't you call the number I gave you?'

Michelle burned with rage. There was no point in remembering the gentle charmer she had met in that sun-drenched French villa. He no longer existed—if he ever had. All the time Alessandro had acted the part of an ordinary man he had been deceiving her. The formidable character sitting opposite her bore no relation to the silver-tongued charmer who had led her astray so easily.

'If I hadn't decided to visit you while I was in the area, I suppose the first I would have heard about this business would have been when you arrived with the child on my doorstep, ready to thrash out the details of a pay-off?'

Aghast, Michelle was stung into a reply. 'No! That was the last thing on my mind!' Calling her pregnancy 'this business' showed only too exactly how he felt. She couldn't stand it, and barely managed to form enough words to explain. 'From the moment I found out I was pregnant I knew I'd have to tell you, Alessandro. And I tried. But you didn't exactly make it easy, did you?'

This was coming out all wrong. Michelle pressed her hands to her face in despair. The loneliness, sickness, uncertainty and downright terror she had suffered over the last few months finally bubbled to the surface. Despite all her best intentions she dissolved, right there in front of him.

With a sigh, Alessandro pulled a brand-new handkerchief from the breast pocket of his suit and handed it to her across the aisle of the jet. Staring resolutely out of the window while she collected herself, he shook his head when she offered it back to him.

'I'm so sorry about it all, Alessandro.'

'I'm sure you are. But not as sorry as our child will be, growing up with coverage of our suspiciously well-timed wedding dragged out of the archives at every opportunity.'

Michelle had been too drenched in her own problems to look that far ahead. When he put it like that, she flared into new life. 'No! I'll do anything to save my baby from being hurt!'

'I'm sure you will.'

In contrast with her dry sobs, Alessandro's voice was unnervingly calm. Unclipping his seat belt, he crossed the distance between them with heavy, measured steps. Michelle willed herself not to shrink away from him as he took the seat beside her. An artist with silken hands had swept her off her feet. Now a tycoon towered over her, the complete master of all the trinkets his lifestyle provided—the executive jet, the gold Rolex, the finest handmade clothes.

As he adjusted his immaculate appearance, one of Alessandro's stewards arrived, carrying a silver tray. Balanced on it was a single glass of chilled champagne and some mineral water.

'You must be thirsty.' Alessandro sat back to let the waiter put down his tray. Michelle gave the man a wan smile. The drinks only served to highlight how far she had been cast adrift from her holiday romance. Alessandro had made breakfast for her at the villa himself, squeezing thick, rich juice from fresh oranges over ice for her to drink. Now a uniformed waiter was opening a sterile bottle and pouring out clear, tasteless liquid.

So much had happened in the past months. When Alessandro left her, back in France, she had felt totally betrayed. He had abandoned her after they shared nothing but tenderness. Today he had plunged back into her life full of accusations, and the press were hounding them both. How could she trust him while things were so bad when he had left her when times were so good?

CHAPTER SEVEN

THE idea that the head of the House of Castiglione might ever let his heart rule his head was one Alessandro wanted to kill straight away. He was still stinging about being compared with his father. He loathed being linked so closely to Sandro Castiglione. In only a few years he had transformed his father's failing business from an old-fashioned art dealership into an international concern.

Alessandro's fortune diverted a constant stream of spoiled beauties through his life. He always made a point of treating women well—until they threatened to get between him and his work. It was a reaction against the way his father had always behaved. In common with most of Alessandro's other relatives, Old Sandro had possessed the morals of a *bracco Italiano* and the loyalty of a cat. He'd treated work as a distraction from his real career of infidelity. Old Sandro had used women as possessions, abandoning them as easily as he had thrown away money.

Alessandro was no prude, but he conducted his own affairs with care and discretion. With one spectacular exception he had always chosen carefully—women who understood his lifestyle. They knew the score. Castiglione men might sample a thousand flowers, but their wives would be chosen from among a tiny caste of the most influential and ancient Tuscan families.

Then this little foreigner had edged her way into his life. With hair the colour of *caramello* and a laugh that acted like balm to his soul, she had made him forget a thousand years of history. From the instant he'd seen her, nothing but the moment had existed for him. They had been two strangers, enjoying a break from real life with no pressure, no commitments and no comeback. Alessandro hadn't given the House of Castiglione a single thought for the whole of his stay at the villa. It had been the perfect summer indulgence—nothing more.

Or so he had thought.

Months later, here they were—together again. Circumstances could not have been more different. He watched Michelle covertly as she sipped her drink. The more he saw of her, the less he liked himself. *It's all my doing,* he thought ruefully. *I took that glorious, sun-kissed creature and turned her into this scared, world-weary woman.*

Trust was a delicate thing. Alessandro knew that only too well. It was why he never offered anyone any more than he could afford to lose. Until now he had always let women come to him and leave when they liked. This girl was unique in that she was the only one he had approached. She was also the only one he had walked away from. The thought of that made him restless.

Something had been working away inside him, like grit in an oyster. It had been nothing more than a minor irritation to begin with, but the feeling had grown day by day. He could pinpoint the exact second it had started.

He shut his eyes and pictured the scene exactly. Swifts had screamed past the helicopter taking him from the yacht to the villa Jolie Fleur. The sky had been Madonna-blue, and the sun so intense it had been no surprise to see her lingering in the shadows. And then it had happened. Alessandro had realised she was trapped, and completely at his mercy. No Italian man with a pulse could have resisted such a delicious opportunity. From that moment on he'd forgotten all about work, and had gone to offer his assistance. When she had turned that wide-eyed loveliness directly on him he'd been lost.

After that, things had gone from bad to disastrous. With a smile and a giggle, Miss Michelle Spicer had slipped under his defences and made him forget every rule. Alessandro's only excuse was that her uncomplicated, easy charm had been so different from any woman he had seduced before. It had made him blind to the dangers. It was exactly those qualities of innocence and gentleness that had made him reach out to her in the garden. And that had been when it had all gone wrong. By not telling him she was a virgin she had deceived him. Her silence had turned his fling into something dishonourable, and confirmed Alessandro's low opinion of women. He had done wrong, but her silence had been worse.

He opened his eyes. What else could he expect? All women were the same. Show them a rich man and they became leeches, out for everything they could get. But Alessandro knew what could happen when neither parent took responsibility for their actions, and he was going to make damned sure it never happened to any child of his. This whole problem was something far more important than either his feelings or Michelle's.

'I am not one of these men who take pride in leaving a trail of bastards wherever I go, Michelle.' His accent thickened as he got ready to confront the subject that was crouching on his shoulder.

Her head whipped around and she stared at him.

He carried on. 'I am interested only in the baby. That innocent child needs a parent with morals and values.'

With a moan of horror, Michelle put her head in her hands. How could he speak to her like this? What had happened to the softly spoken man who had taken her to paradise? He had changed, turning from a lover into a mean-minded monster. This was no longer a rescue but an entrapment. She needed to escape—sooner rather than later.

'I can't take any more of this.' She flapped her hands, desperately searching for the handkerchief he'd given her earlier. Finding it, she scrubbed her face dry and confronted him. 'The moment we land, I want you to put me on a plane going straight back to England!'

Alessandro picked up the fine lead-crystal glass before him. Turning it slightly, he inspected his champagne's filigree of tiny bubbles.

'No. You're coming with me to my villa. As I said, if you are claiming the right to be the mother of my child, you must take the responsibility of becoming my wife. A guest wing is being made ready for you right now. It will be perfect by the time we arrive.' He took a sip, and smiled appreciatively at the taste of his favourite vintage.

Michelle blinked at him. 'Then you were serious when you called me your fiancée?' she said in a whisper.

'I would never joke about something like that.'

'But what if I refuse?'

Alessandro drained his glass and called for a refill. 'You won't, if you're a clever girl and listen to reason. I need an heir. You have my child. Marry me and I will support you and care for you and the baby from now on, no questions asked. Refuse, and I will have that child the moment it is born. I would rather avoid scandal, Michelle, but not at the expense on my child. My legal team will ensure you never see it again, or one penny of compensation.'

His eyes were blazing. Michelle was terrified, but she could not go down without a fight.

'Mothers have rights, too,' she said staunchly, her hand moving nervously over her stomach.

'If it wasn't for the generosity of my charitable foundation you wouldn't have a job or a home. A condition of your tenancy at Rose Cottage and the gallery is honesty. You withheld from me the fact that I was to become a father. That means you'll lose both, in case the press decide you got the job and the house by blackmailing me. No court in the world would leave a child to grow up homeless with an unemployed mother. Not when the alternative is better in every single way,' he finished acidly.

Michelle didn't need to dwell on her own miserable childhood to recognise that truth. Her only hope was to appeal against the scorn in his eyes.

'Alessandro, how can I stay in your home, let alone marry you, when all you face me with is accusations?

What basis for a relationship is that? If you're deaf to the truth then there's no point spending any more time together than we must.'

'I told you back in the summer—I'm not interested in a relationship with you. But there is every point in the two of us presenting a united front, Michelle. Remember the international press filling your little street in England? That was a picnic compared with what you will face in *Italia*. There, the paparazzi are on home ground. My estate in Tuscany is secure. They don't bother me. It is my own private haven from them. But for a woman who refuses my protection—well, I couldn't guarantee anything.'

His words were almost a threat. Michelle looked at him, but his expression was impassive.

'All those people back in Market Street will have gone by now. They'll have forgotten about me,' she said with an attempt at defiance. 'They'll have found a new scoop.'

'No.' Alessandro shook his head, and all his authority escaped in that single word.

As he put his glass down on the table in front of them the champagne inside it shivered. So did Michelle.

'That's not the way the international press works when a member of the Castiglione family is at the heart of the drama. For the past two years *I* have been the House of Castiglione. Me! I have turned it from a laughing stock into a respectable institution. Because of that, everything I do is news in my own country—which is good for my family's company as long as the publicity is of the right sort. I don't intend to jeopardise the lives and careers of all the people who work for me because the press turns your little drama into a full-blown scandal. You have a choice.'

His kept his voice level, but it was crackling with reproach.

'If you add to the media frenzy by making a scene when we land, or refuse the protection I can give you at the Villa Castiglione, it will guarantee they follow your every movement from now on.'

All the arguments Michelle had been itching to voice died on her lips. The thought of exciting any more attention was truly chilling. All she wanted to do was disappear and keep her baby safe. There was no way she would willingly throw herself into the jaws of the press.

When they reached the airport, Alessandro's party was fast-tracked through the formalities.

'Where's my luggage?' Michelle looked round in panic, remembering the queues and confusion of her one other trip abroad.

'I'm surprised you ask,' Alessandro said with grim humour. 'You'll never need to worry about anything like that again. It's all being dealt with. You aren't the housekeeper any longer, Michelle.' He took a firm grip on her elbow and guided her towards a private exit. 'Forget it. Just concentrate on smiling, in case a stray cameraman spots us.'

Tuscan sunshine gleamed on the glassy surface of a sleek black sports car waiting for them outside. Alessandro, always preferring to drive himself, had made sure it was dropped off earlier by a member of his staff. Opening the door, Alessandro waited until Michelle was settled before going round to the driver's seat.

'Here comes a photographer. And where there's one, there will be others,' he explained with a heavy sigh, and he was right.

He had to slalom the car around the figures leaping off the pavement, trying to make them slow down. Everyone was desperate for a taste of Alessandro's action.

'They're like ants.' He hit the switch that darkened the car's windows.

Michelle was glad no one could see in, but as the car threw off its pursuers and moved out onto a main road she wished she could see out. Pressing one of the buttons on her armrest, she lowered the window beside her.

'Why not use the air-conditioning?' Alessandro said as the glass slid down silently to let hot, dry air whip around the car's interior.

'I wanted to see out,' she said. 'This is lovely,' she breathed as the amber and gold countryside of Italy sped past outside.

'It's hard not to love it here,' Alessandro said in a voice heavy with irony.

He drove smoothly and powerfully, and Michelle found his silent efficiency amazing and strangely appealing. She had only known him as an artist, with talent in his fingertips. Now he mastered the car with effortless ease. It was difficult to keep her eyes off him. Although the timeless landscape outside tugged at her attention, she could not look away from the man who had come back into her life so suddenly. His personality filled the car, and she could feel her body respond to his closeness. Alessandro was impossible to ignore.

Eventually he turned off the main carriageway and continued along a series of winding lanes. Rolling hectares of farmland on either side of the road became hemmed with small fields and stone walls. The road began to climb, and Michelle saw a small village clinging to the hillside ahead.

'That's where we're heading. The other side of the valley is prettier.'

His words were prophetic. The small stone walls on either side of the lane suddenly grew taller, until the car was running through shadowy canyons. Ancient multi-storeyed houses reared up, shutting out the sun. Geraniums spilled down from every ledge, doing their best to cheer the roadside homes, but it was an uphill struggle. Finally he pulled in and stopped.

'We're here,' Alessandro said simply.

Michelle sat up straight in her seat. They were parked in front of a large pair of metal gates. As Alessandro keyed a security code into an intercom, she tried to take everything in. This part of the road was in deep shade, made all the more sinister by towering evergreens leering over the top of the wall. It looked like the entrance to a cemetery. Michelle's spirits had never been very high. Now they sank with her, back into her seat. Only when the automatic gates swung open could she dare to hope again.

Her first glimpse of Alessandro's world was stunning. A broad, mile-long drive was hemmed on either side by an avenue of shady lime trees. Between their trunks Michelle glimpsed parallel lines of vines hugging the rolling contours of Alessandro's estate. The end of each row billowed with roses, their lissom banners of pink and white flowers making a vivid contrast with the rigidly trained grapes.

'It's beautiful. Absolutely beautiful,' she whispered. 'Look how the vine leaves are turning red already!'

'Yes…' Alessandro mused, as though noticing for the first time how autumn was searing the foliage. 'The cold nights and low sun make it happen every year at about this time.'

Michelle shot a quick glance at him across the car's interior. He scanned his surroundings, and then returned his focus to the road ahead. Disappointed, she tried to recapture her first flare of excitement at the scene outside. It didn't take long. Ancient chestnut woodland softened much of the Castiglione estate, but there were enough pines and cypresses standing guard on the horizon to remind her that this was the real Tuscany. He was driving towards a large, rambling villa perched on an outcrop of rock. Golden stone and terracotta tiles gave it an apricot glow in the soft afternoon light. As the car growled up the dusty carriageway it became obvious that they really were heading straight for the palace on the rock.

Michelle gasped. 'Good grief—is that your home?'

'It's where I live—for some of the time, at least. You're impressed?' Alessandro sounded surprised.

'Of course I am. I've never seen anything like this before. The South of France was my one and only trip out of England.' She was craning her neck, twisting in her seat to see as much of the vast estate as possible. 'Did you ever build the artist's studio you wanted?'

He shook his head. 'Not yet. It will be a wrench to change from the building I've used for so long. You can't see that from here. It's at the far side of the estate, to make sure I can control who goes there.'

Take a look at what's on offer at

www.millsandboon.co.uk

⌐⟍

MILLS & BOON
Pure reading pleasure

My Account / Offer of the Month / Our Authors / Book Club / Contact us

All of the latest books are there **PLUS**

⊚ Free Online reads

⊚ Exclusive offers and competitions

⊚ At least **15%** discount on our huge back list

⊚ Sign up to our free monthly eNewsletter

⊚ More info on your favourite authors

⊚ **Browse the Book** to try before you buy

⊚ eBooks available for most titles

⊚ Join the M&B community and **discuss** your favourite books with other readers

Search I Countries I Affiliates I Site Map I Company Information I Careers I Privacy Policy I Terms and Conditions I Aspiring Authors I Submit Manuscript I FAQs
Copyright © 2000 - 2008 Harlequin Mills & Boon Limited* All rights reserved.

Take a look at what's on offer at

www.millsandboon.co.uk

His terse reply brought Michelle up short. It was as though this new, unfamiliar Alessandro was trying to shut her out of the best part of his world. Resentment led her to make an equally acid retort.

'I suppose that means you only use it to entertain people who aren't as grand as you?'

'No. I go there to be alone.' His reply ricocheted back to her. 'My working days are crammed full of people and problems. My studio isn't. Unless I invite them.'

Their car was approaching the villa's entrance. There couldn't have been a greater contrast between the little studio house in France and this gracious collection of buildings. The original, ancient villa had been extended over centuries. It was now a rambling wonderland of tiles, towers and balconies. The car came to a halt in a big cobbled yard, overlooked on every side by dozens of windows. Each one spilled waves of glowing scarlet geraniums over the ancient stonework. It was a startling farewell to summer, but Michelle was in no mood to appreciate her surroundings any more.

'If you feel like that, Alessandro, then I'm amazed you let *me* into your secret world.'

'At the time I thought more of you than I do now.'

Before Michelle had time to think of a reply, Alessandro got out of the car and walked around to open the door for her. As he did so she looked up, first into the closed mystery of his face and then at the towering glory of his ancestral home. Both made her very aware of her insignificance. When staff surrounded the car and began unloading the luggage from its boot it was final proof that Alessandro's lifestyle was as far removed from hers as it was possible to get. It was an awful lot to take in.

One foot poised over the cobblestones, she hesitated. 'This place is enormous!'

Alessandro was in no mood to linger. He caught hold of her hand and drew her out of the car. The smooth, firm touch of his skin was at first reassuring, but his unsettling gaze was too much for her. To her alarm, a tingle of something she had almost forgotten shot straight through her body. With growing warmth she recognised it as physical arousal. She tried to draw back, but Alessandro refused to let her.

'I'm sure a clever girl like you will soon get used to it. Now we must eat. I'll take you to your rooms while my staff take care of everything else. There will be time for a guided tour later on—but only if you're not too tired.'

The mention of food did something strange to Michelle's stomach. It began to whirl as fast as her brain. Things had been moving far too fast. Alessandro might think he'd been gracious in giving her a choice of struggling on alone in England or being overwhelmed in Italy. In reality, his alternatives gave her no choice at all. The height of the surrounding walls, the size of his house and estate were incredible, and those great gates were a comfort. All the same, they made her feel like a bird in a gilded cage. The thought made her light-headed, but before she could decide if her situation was good or bad a more unwelcome feeling arrived to overwhelm her.

'Michelle? What is it? Are you all right?' Alessandro's voice was dark with concern as he stopped and turned to face her.

She tried breathing slowly and deeply. Sometimes it could delay the inevitable. This time it didn't work.

'Do you have a bathroom?' Swallowing hard, she got the words out somehow.

Lifting her into his arms, Alessandro carried her into the villa. Half a dozen of his long strides got them to a door at the side of the entrance hall. He carried her through into a smartly spartan office, and throwing open the door of an executive washroom, placed her down carefully.

'This must be one of the benefits of working from home,' he muttered as she made a dash for the lavatory.

That it should come to this, she thought. *I'm crumpled on a strange floor in a foreign country.* Her shame surely couldn't get any worse. For a sophisticated man like Alessandro, this must be the worst possible lapse in behaviour.

When it was over, she struggled slowly back to life. Behind her, someone was running a tap. As her vision cleared she could see exactly how luxurious this bathroom was. The walls and floor were covered in sea-green marble. It provided the perfect background for all the gold fitments, and the cold, white porcelain she had been so glad to lean against. It was then that her focus steadied on the highly polished black shoes inches from her. She followed the impeccable knife-edged creases of Alessandro's smart suit and realised he had come to her rescue with another welcome glass of water.

'I—I'm sorry, Alessandro…' Too weak and wretched to stand, she drained the glass while still sitting on the floor of his executive bathroom.

'I thought it was supposed to be morning sickness,' he said calmly.

'So did I.' Her reply was heartfelt. 'The past few

weeks have shown me otherwise. It can happen at any time during the day or night.'

'I'll get my doctor to give you something.'

'No…I'd rather not.' She shook her head, wincing at the rawness of her throat. 'I haven't taken so much as a paracetamol since I found out about the baby. I don't want to start now.'

'Are you sure?' Alessandro searched her face.

Despite the feeling she had been turned inside out both physically and mentally, she nodded.

'That's good.' He nodded appreciatively and took the glass from her hands. 'You look exhausted. You should rest while you can. I'll take you straight up to your room. My doctor will be sent for—' He was already keying a number into his mobile, but Michelle held up her hand.

'There's no need, really. I'm feeling better already. It was probably all the travelling, and the fact I haven't eaten since breakfast.'

He muttered something in Italian, and then patted her shoulder absently. 'My mistake—I should have insisted you ate more. And you'll be too tired for visitors today, by the time you've settled in. I'll tell the doctor to call first thing in the morning. Merely as a formality, you understand, as I agree with you. You shouldn't take anything beyond the best food and drink—only the best *Italian* sort, of course—while you are carrying the Castiglione heir.'

Somehow his words managed to make Michelle feel better and worse at the same time. Everything was being taken out of her hands. She had no say in anything any more. While the baby played havoc with her body,

Alessandro was putting himself in charge of every other detail. She knew she should have been glad of the help. Instead, the last few troubled hours all crowded in on her at once. The long, stressful day, the travelling and her unruly hormones dragged her down into the depths of despair. Pushing her sweat-damp hair back from her face, she couldn't hold back her feelings any longer.

'I never wanted this to happen,' she said softly.

Alessandro sighed. 'It happens.'

Slipping his hands around her waist, he lifted her carefully to her feet. Michelle felt so weak and wobbly she couldn't avoid leaning against him. She expected him to recoil at such a pathetic show. After all, he had been in a towering rage from the moment he strode back into her life that morning. But instead of pushing her off he stood firm. Tension kept his body rigid, and his arm dropped onto her shoulder rather than enfolding her, but at least he made the gesture. Michelle guessed it was the only support she could expect, and she was grateful for it. She closed her eyes and tried to forget everything else but her baby.

'After everything that's happened, how can I put things right, Alessandro? You say you want to improve your family's reputation, but when the baby comes early everyone will know we *had* to get married!'

'I will deal with it.'

'How?' She gazed up at him as he helped her through his office and out into the entrance hall again. His jaw was a resolute line.

'I employ the top PR team in the country. Press exclusives come and go, but the House of Castiglione must go on for ever.'

There was such an unusual edge to his voice that Michelle couldn't bear to ask what he meant. As though reading her mind, he closed his hand over hers. It had all the warmth and gentleness that was missing from his expression and voice, but the feeling lasted only seconds. After a fleeting squeeze he let go, and guided her in the direction of a grand marble staircase.

'I'll deal with it,' he repeated firmly.

CHAPTER EIGHT

MICHELLE wished she could feel relieved at Alessandro's words. Instead, she became more confused than ever. This whole disaster had come about because she had put all her faith in him once before. Knowing what she knew now, it would be a leap of faith to trust him to sort anything out. And as for marrying him…!

She was shattered—physically, mentally and emotionally—and no longer knew what to think. There had been one new experience after another, and now she hardly had the strength or will to put one foot in front the other. When a maid hurried up with a smile and an unintelligible question, it was the last straw. She burst into tears.

Alessandro dismissed the girl with a nod of his head. He waited until they were alone again before speaking.

'What is the matter, Michelle?' His questioning was cool and offhand.

'I c-couldn't understand what she said…she wasn't speaking English…' she blurted out between sobs.

'Why should she?' Alessandro lifted a quizzical eyebrow. 'You're in Italy now. You'll need to learn our language. But don't worry. I'll get someone to teach you.' He batted her problem away with a casual gesture.

The last thing Michelle wanted right now was lessons. She found it hard enough speaking to this new, dynamic Alessandro. The idea of having to work with a tutor in a foreign language brought back all her worst memories of math lessons at school. Her tears kept coming. With a long-suffering sigh, Alessandro found the handkerchief he had given her once before and put it into her hands.

'Couldn't you teach me?' She sniffed into its folds.

He shrugged off her suggestion. 'I don't spend enough time here. As I told you, the Villa Castiglione is my retreat from business life. I'm often away for long periods.'

'So I'm going to be left here on my own?'

'There are worse places,' he reminded her with a glance that took in the sunlit hallway. It was lined with antique furniture and priceless works of art—a silent oasis of calm. 'Market Street filled with paparazzi, *per esempio*.'

Michelle didn't need to speak Italian to understand the veiled threat behind his words. *If you don't like it here, you can go back to all that.* She tried to challenge him with a stare, but it was impossible. Her eyes were too red and raw. The golden light flooding in from the windows overlooking an inner courtyard made him seem more aloof and aristocratic than ever. It cast his eyes in mystery, and emphasised the feeling that he could bring emotional shutters clanging down against her at any time he liked. Appealing against any decision he made would be like banging her fists against a brick wall.

She could do nothing but follow in silence as he led her upstairs towards one of the villa's guest wings.

* * *

Alessandro's childhood had taught him emotions were a weakness. As far as he could see, strong men could not afford them. That had become his reality. His true feelings were so deeply buried that he barely knew they existed. But Michelle had nearly achieved the impossible. Several times he had almost told her exactly what he thought about gold-diggers who manipulated circumstances to suit themselves. Then she'd turned those big, limpid brown eyes on him. Every time the words had died on his lips. God, the girl could act. He had been completely taken in by her soft words and seduction in the summer, but it wouldn't happen again.

As he led Michelle past statues and priceless paintings on the way to her suite, he tried to concentrate on his surroundings. When she pointed out exactly how lovely the old place was he made a mental note not to take anything for granted any more. He realised how rarely he took the time to really look around him nowadays.

The Villa Castiglione was the nearest thing Alessandro had to a home—although, in view of his tempestuous past, 'home' was too cosy a word for it. Visitors to the place made him uneasy. It was like exposing a raw nerve. Bringing Michelle here was difficult, but he felt it was the least he could do. No parent should be expected to raise a child alone.

He told himself he should be glad she'd accepted so meekly. He wasn't a bully by nature, and disliked having to force her in any way. The memory of those few delicious summer days they'd shared was still so sweet and fresh in his mind and he wanted to keep it there. Michelle had been so unspoiled, so willing. Everything about her was so inviting—especially, he thought with a lurch of lust, her body.

He cast a sidelong glance at her as they walked along the villa's upper gallery.

'You are looking better,' he observed.

'It comes and goes.'

Like a woman's loyalty, he thought to himself, managing not to let memory taint his expression. Today Michelle looked even more impressive than he remembered, with her breasts cupped invitingly by a close-fitting top. It clung to her perfectly. He could see where her natural softness spilled over the firm outline of her bra. The thought of cradling that pale tenderness in his hands again unleashed a tidal wave of desire in him. But even as Alessandro managed to restrain himself he knew it was going to be tricky.

Each time they passed one of the indoor staff heads were inclined towards Michelle, as though she was royalty. Despite the long, infuriating day, Alessandro found himself smiling at her reaction. She was delighted every time. He liked that, despite the current circumstances. After all, pleasing women was one of his favourite pastimes.

Alessandro's expression clouded only once as he guided her along the gallery towards her rooms. It was when he felt the thrum of the PDA in his pocket. He killed the call without answering it.

Recently voted the world's most outstanding entrepreneur, Alessandro had succeeded by being ruthless. The tribe of Castiglione hadn't believed any Italian man worth the name would sack his own relatives, but he had done it. The least he could do for the family after that was marry a good Tuscan girl, they'd argued—and by that they meant one of his cousins. He was supposed to raise *bambini*, secure the future of the House of Castiglione, and keep them all in jobs for life.

Alessandro's finely sculpted nostrils flared at the mere thought of it. He'd never taken orders from anyone in his life, and he wasn't about to start now. He owed his extended family nothing. And when he remembered the way his father had always treated him—

'Alessandro? Are you all right?'

'What?' Emerging from his waking nightmare, Alessandro looked down at Michelle. Focussing on her sweet, apprehensive smile reminded him of why she was here in his sanctuary.

The Castigliones want an heir to the family firm. Well, here it is, he thought bitterly.

He shrugged. '*Certo*, Michelle. I was thinking about work, that's all.'

'Oh, I know exactly what you mean,' Michelle said with a rush of feeling.

Her response was so heartfelt Alessandro laughed. He couldn't stop himself. It was the first time in weeks he had done anything like that. They glanced at each other, exchanging a look of shared suffering. For one single second the magic of understanding united them. Michelle's eyes widened, but her own laughter died before she could make a sound. Her lips parted in a way that told Alessandro work was suddenly the very last thing on her mind.

His desire for her rose up again, threatening to rip off his mask of civilisation. He needed to kiss her senseless right there in the gallery, to run his hands over her warm soft skin, to carry her to his bed and make love to her all night long—

That won't solve anything! he told himself sharply. Using sex to block out painful memories had never helped him in the past. But even as he felt the need to try the easy route to oblivion, Alessandro became aware of a new and shocking truth. For the first time in his life he admitted to himself that sex on its own would never be enough to dull his pain.

He wanted someone to take away the terrible hollow feeling that echoed right through him.

Trapped by the look in his eyes, Michelle could not move. His gaze ran over her like quicksilver. He used it, and her reaction, with practised skill. The touch of his fingers could not have affected her more. His expression played her as though she were a priceless violin. It made her want him. But all the time she knew from experience that once this man started something there could be no going back…

At that moment a strand of Michelle's hair fell free from the ponytail she was wearing to keep it away from her face. With a slow, calculated movement, Alessandro reached out and brushed it back behind her ear.

'It still feels like silk,' he murmured, leaning in close so she could catch the longing behind his words. When he spoke again, his voice was as sweet and low as a stream in summer. 'I was curious—I thought pregnancy might force all sorts of changes on your body.'

His gaze was as intense as ever. Michelle could feel it as surely as the whisper of his breath against her skin. In an instant she realised he was going to kiss her. Anticipation crackled through the air like an electric charge. Irresistibly drawn towards him, she closed her eyes, waiting for his touch. Fatigue, resentment, loneliness… She forgot everything. This was going to be heavenly. The sound of her heart pounded insistently in her ears, making her dizzy.

Then she felt Alessandro hesitate, as something outside their little bubble of solitude caught his eye. In that second a formal greeting echoed through the gallery. It was a maid, rustling up with a message for him. In response he laughed, and the spell was broken. Michelle had to stand by and watch Alessandro and his staff member smile and chat away easily in their own language. It meant nothing to her. She felt painfully isolated.

Her job done, the maid walked away without turning a hair. All the staff acted as though Alessandro escorted young women through his villa all the time—which, Michelle reminded herself sharply, he probably did.

'Your rooms are ready.' Alessandro's tone was back to business—they were strangers again.

As they reached the end of the corridor Alessandro opened a great oak door.

'Welcome to your suite, Michelle. I'm sure you'll be happy here.'

She had a sudden vision of being just another girl in Alessandro's regular parade of female guests. Her face twisted with cynicism—but only until she saw inside the door he was holding open for her. All her doubts vanished the moment he stepped aside for her to go in.

She had expected nothing more than a simple bedroom, with possibly an *en suite* bathroom. What she found was a large, sunlit room with comfortable seats and a table—and this was only the reception area. On the far side a glazed door gave a glimpse of a wide colonnaded walkway beyond. That led to one of the villa's towers a few metres away. Alessandro led her over to the door and opened it for her. Michelle crossed the threshold, but only took a couple of steps before stopping.

'Go ahead. What are you waiting for?' he prompted.

Michelle was too busy gazing at the scenery to answer straight away. The loggia overlooked slopes spread out below the villa, and it felt like being on top of the world. 'The view…it's breathtaking!' she gasped.

'Careful—it's a long way down.' Alessandro shadowed her as she went to lean on the loggia's wide stone sill.

He was right. The villa's hilltop position meant the ground fell away alarmingly. Michelle was careful not to look straight down—that would have been too much for her delicate stomach. Instead, she gazed across the valley's chestnut woods. Autumn was already spinning gold through the leaves.

'Are you cold?'

'No, I'm fine.'

It was Michelle's turn to frown. She had been so careful not to let him see her shiver. How had he known? Then with alarm she realised what had tipped him off.

Letting go of the balcony, she raised her hands to clasp them in front of her, trying to hide the buds of her nipples. She had been enjoying the tingle of their arousal pressing against the lace of her bra, but his gaze was too appreciative. Her body simmered with an illicit longing to feel his touch again, but he already thought the worst of her. She wasn't about to confirm his suspicions. A flare of colour ran straight to her cheeks.

Alessandro gave her a knowing smile, then moved away along the walkway.

'Let's carry on into the tower. It sounds like dinner is ready.'

His hearing must be as acute as his eyesight, Michelle thought as he gestured towards the far end of the loggia.

She had been given the whole of one of the villa's fairy-tale towers as her temporary home. A sunny sitting room led out onto a terrace with more breathtaking views of the beautiful countryside. That wasn't the only surprise. A uniformed maid was setting out a meal for two inside a conservatory banked with flowers. It had been designed as an intimate dining area for when chill breezes ran up the valley. Here, the fragrance of citrus bushes and peppery cyclamen mingled with the oriental spices of their meal. On a table just large enough for two, silver salvers had been covered with a wonderful display of salads and titbits that would have tempted the most reluctant diner.

'Today has been a bad experience for us both, Michelle. Let's sit down, enjoy a good meal and take stock.'

He pulled out one of the delicate wrought-iron chairs for her to take a seat. Michelle's appetite did one of its now familiar U-turns. Looking at the food revived her. She couldn't help giggling nervously as she took her place. Twenty-four hours ago she had been eating egg and chips from a tray in front of a portable television set. Now Alessandro Castiglione, billionaire business-man, was entertaining her at a table filled with exotic hand-made treats. He looked good enough to eat, and so did her stunning surroundings.

This is the perfect setting for seduction, she thought with a painful pang. That set all sorts of alarm bells ringing. Michelle knew she ought to be on her guard. She had already given Alessandro everything. He had responded by abandoning her. Yet the knowledge that his thigh was only inches away from hers beneath the table was pushing that episode right out of her mind...

'This is just a taste of what my chefs can do. Let me know what you like, and I'll make sure it's on the menu,' Alessandro said as he picked up one of the silver dishes and handed it to her. Their fingers touched as she took it, and he smiled.

It was the simplest of gestures, but the expressive look in his eyes told Michelle more than words ever could. He was weighing up the difficult situation, too.

'I don't eat much these days,' Michelle said, scooping a tiny portion of tabbouleh onto her plate. She was starving, but wasn't sure nerves would let her eat. And it would be unthinkable to leave anything on her plate at a time like this.

Alessandro regarded her sharply as he offered some fresh orange salad.

'You must. Everything that goes into your mouth should do the baby good. You're lucky to be in such a position of influence over its health and welfare.'

Michelle cringed. His mention of their child was nothing more than a device to make her do the right thing. She accepted the salad, but knew she had to divert him onto some other subject. False interest in her well-being was the last thing she needed.

'And *you're* lucky to live in a place like this!' she said brightly. 'It must have been so lovely for you to grow up here. Lots of servants to do all the chores, and no need to worry about getting good grades in school.'

She looked at the metalwork forming the conservatory's glazed roof. It was as light as lace. The architecture here was as stunning as the food and flowers.

'Luck has nothing to do with it. It was my misfortune to be born here, but I made the best of the hand life dealt me.'

Michelle's mouth dropped open. It was an outrageous view of his privileged life, but Alessandro was too busy creating his meal to notice the effect his words were having on her. He carried on talking.

'The only reason I am rich is because I work hard. This place has nothing to do with the House of Castiglione. Rather, it is my sanctuary from it.'

His arm brushed lightly against hers as they both reached for the same dish. She immediately retreated.

'After you.' Alessandro nodded.

The gesture was as straightforward as his words, and Michelle realised that when Alessandro was on form, what you saw was what you got. He might have faults, but false modesty wasn't one of them. Her heart began to accelerate at the thought of his other vices. *How many other women have been entertained right here, like this?* she wondered. *And what happened to them afterwards?* Watching Alessandro in his natural habitat made her temperature rise. She put down her cutlery. How could anyone think of eating at a time like this?

He took her hesitancy as a hint, and dropped a couple of tiny filo parcels onto her plate.

'If we're to marry, Alessandro,' she said slowly, 'I ought to learn something about you.'

'You could have done that a lot sooner by phoning the contact number I left in my note,' he said coolly.

Indignation flared in Michelle's cheeks. 'I tried—believe me! When I rang, your secretary refused to put me through to you. I overheard her say "It's another one!" to someone else in the office. I took that to mean you give all your women the same number, knowing they'll never get past your firewall of lackeys!' she finished in a rush.

There was a long and threatening silence. When Alessandro eventually replied, it was with such cold venom that Michelle actually shrank in her seat.

'So you think I'm the kind of man who lies to women, do you?' He held her eyes with his as he took a fork and stabbed at his meal. 'Let me tell you, Michelle, I consider that the worst form of deceit.'

She looked away, trying to hide the pain as she recalled the happier times they had spent together. Honesty clearly had a different meaning for Alessandro.

'You were so unlike all the other people I'd worked for—so *ordinary* when we first met! Now I discover you've got a million staff, a private plane, different cars in every country and apartments all over the world—' She brought herself up sharply. She didn't want him to think she was obsessed with the perks of his jet-set lifestyle. Alessandro already imagined she might try and take advantage of him. If he thought she'd been reading up on him in the glossy magazines, he might think she was out to make something from her situation. 'I mean, you've told me you have to travel a lot for your work, of course…' she finished lamely.

'The House of Castiglione is a good enough reason

to keep me on the move,' he agreed, flashing the briefest of smiles. 'But there's more to it than that. As I've told you before, I don't like to be tied down—either by people or places.'

The atmosphere eased, but despite that twitch of his lips there was no amusement left in Alessandro's expression. His words were clearly meant as a warning, but the nearness of him was a reminder of the pleasure they'd shared. It was as if he sensed the depth of her attraction for him but refused to give her any encouragement—quite the opposite, in fact.

Michelle struggled to concentrate on her food. Her mind was befuddled. She felt as though Alessandro was a master hypnotist. He could convince her of one thing, and then wake her suddenly from a dream to tell her something else.

He continued with all the smooth assurance of a professional host. 'Before I inherited my father's business concerns I made myself successful on my own account. I left school as soon as I could, got a job at a burger place and worked my way up to become managing director.'

'You worked in fast food?' Michelle gasped, her own situation temporarily forgotten. She could hardly believe it.

He shrugged off her amazement with a hollow laugh. 'I wanted to prove myself in a field where no one could say I'd traded on my family's name. So that's exactly what I did. While I was in charge the place went from an also-ran to the market leader, and won any number of nutritional awards.'

That was some achievement. Michelle was ultracautious when it came to food. The chain produced the only type of burgers she would eat. It was amazing that Alessandro could take something so commonplace and mould it into such a success.

She thought back to her own unhappy childhood. 'Your parents must be very proud of you.'

'Ha—*neanche per sogno*!' He snorted, but almost as soon as he had done so a strange expression came over his face. 'Anyway, they're both dead now. But if you read the gossip columns you would surely know that? They would also have taught you my father was the most generous of men…but only with money. When it came to love and loyalty—'

He stopped abruptly. Picking up his knife and fork, he carried on with his meal. His movements were in such contrast with his usual one-handed Italian ease that Michelle knew she was looking into an open wound. She needed to know more, but sensed it was safer to change the subject.

'You had your mother to give you that security, I suppose.' Michelle sighed. Other people always did. It was a pain she suffered every time conversation got around to family life.

'I never had a real mother.'

There was a strange lack of feeling in his words. Michelle picked up on it straight away and looked at him sharply.

'Oh, Alessandro, I'm so sorry.'

He raised his head to look at her. Once again she saw the guards in place in his expression. *He's slammed down those shutters against me again*, she thought, but he waved away her concern.

'It trained me to succeed. When I was catapulted

into the top job at the House of Castiglione nothing changed. And everything.'

Alessandro wasn't the only one who could change the subject to good effect. Michelle grabbed the chance to steer their conversation away from parental pain. She had suffered enough of that herself. It was good to realise she wasn't unique, but this wasn't the place for post-mortems.

'You went straight from fast food to fine art? That's quite a contrast!' she said, awestruck. 'How did you manage the switch?'

'It wasn't a problem.' Alessandro dismissed her question with a casual shrug of one shoulder. 'I had spent my whole time fighting to improve international fast food. To me, quality is everything. Pace is nothing. Going to work for the House of Castiglione was like leaving a busy *piazza* and walking into an ancient cathedral. It's possible to appreciate both, at the right time and in the right circumstances.'

'And you struck lucky?'

Alessandro put down his knife and picked up a decanter of wine. It glistened like blood as he poured himself a glass before replying. 'I don't believe in luck. All my life I've forged my own success, without the help of anyone or anything. Don't you say in English, *he travels fastest who travels alone*?'

Michelle could hardly believe what she was hearing. All her life she'd thought she was the only person who'd had to spend every second of every day proving themselves. Now she knew differently. She had always been so desperate for approval there had been no room for anything in her life beyond working for her mother. It sounded as though Alessandro had similar demons. She stared at him in disbelief.

'People who say things like that are usually lonely. But you're so confident, so successful! You can't be lonely—' She looked him directly in the face, trying to see if they had something else in common. 'Can you, Alessandro?'

He took a sip of his drink, taking his time to replace the glass carefully in front of his plate. Resting his elbows on the table, he netted his fingers and rested his chin against them as he considered his answer.

'That's a very personal question. Did I ever ask *you* why you felt able to leave England so soon after your mother's death?' he asked.

Until that moment Michelle had been gazing at him in wonder. Now she looked back to her meal.

'I don't think we'd better go there. My mother would have died of shame to think I'd become the sort of girl who got pregnant on holiday.' She stopped, conscious of straying into an area that should be out of bounds to them both—at least for a while longer.

Alessandro took the initiative. 'Your mother can't possibly have any influence over you any more, Michelle.' He sat back in his seat, surveying her. 'She's gone, and you're a big girl now.'

His eyes roved over her face. Beneath the table she felt his leg briefly make contact with hers. The touch of his expensively tailored trousers against her sent a shock wave straight through her body. Was it an accident? The seductive glimmer in those graphite eyes of his reminded her that Alessandro Castiglione was a man who never made an unconsidered move.

'Maybe,' she answered, uncertain on several counts.

His next move convinced her. As he leaned forward, his wintry expression melted into something close to a smile. 'You have proved yourself woman enough to carry my heir, Michelle. And right now that's the only thing that matters to me. The only thing.'

His movements began speaking directly to her. The long, artistic fingers of his left hand were stroking the damask tablecloth. The relish he took over the action was unmistakable. When he regarded her with those devastating dark eyes, it was with an intimacy she didn't need to question.

'You'd be surprised if you knew what I was really like,' she muttered, breaking eye contact to pour herself a glass of iced water from the carafe standing between them.

She needed it. Alessandro was sending her temperature right off the scale. Was that faint hissing she could hear the air-conditioning, or the surge of her unruly hormones? It was hard to tell. Her mind was reeling with the possibility that any moment now he might reach forward—and she would be there for him. There could be no question about it—

Her self-control was a hair's breadth from shattering completely. She *had* to stop herself anticipating his touch! She *had* to shift the subject onto something unsexy, before all those memories of the first kisses they had shared came back to haunt her again.

'I—I suppose you bring all your sophisticated friends here to the villa?' she began, and then gave herself a mental kick. *Idiot! Now he'll automatically compare me with them!*

'Only the ones who interest me get as far as visiting

this place. And they're as rare as intelligence in the circles I move in. None have been invited to stay in any of the guest suites until now.'

Alessandro poured himself a glass of water and took a sip, moving with an easy assurance that took her breath away. She couldn't escape from his mesmerising eyes. The cast of his features always made her want to reach out and touch him. Her body was reacting to him as surely as if his gaze had been the playful caress of his lips or fingertips. Warmth stole up from her belly, keeping her nipples proud with excitement. She could feel the blood dancing through her veins like champagne. The welcome warmth of arousal made her shift slightly in her seat.

Alessandro lazily impaled some *amori* salad on his fork, but paused before lifting it off the plate. 'Beautiful women, paintings, sculpture…I take an interest in them all, but fine art has always been my first love.'

'You must really enjoy working for an international art dealership like the House of Castiglione,' Michelle said, wondering if she was on solid ground again. Somehow she doubted it. Being so close to him, and knowing not many other people had made it this far, would make it hard to come down to earth ever again.

'I enjoy my work, yes. But the people I work with? That's another matter.' He ate the pasta, then stabbed a roasted cherry tomato. When he had finished that morsel, he tapped his fork on his plate, making the fine china ring. 'Wherever there is money, envy and pain are always close behind.'

'You don't need to tell me that.' Michelle shook her head sorrowfully. She thought of the car she had saved up for so long to buy the previous year. Until she'd got it home she had imagined the worst part of living in a house with no garage would be increased insurance premiums. To find the waterproof cover of her pride and joy slashed on the first night, its paintwork keyed and the wheels stolen was something she still hadn't come to terms with.

'Everyone wants to know me now I've become head of the House of Castiglione. Unfortunately, it is for all the wrong reasons.' Alessandro grimaced.

'I'm sure that isn't true.'

He guffawed. 'That could only be said by a woman who doesn't feel the need to impress anyone.'

Alessandro threw his answer at her in a way that made sure he didn't have to open up any further. This stonewalling only made Michelle want to reach out to him again. She could identify with so many of the things he said. Now she was convinced this beautiful, strangely guarded man would haunt her until the end of time. She also knew she didn't need to tell him that. A sea of admiration must surround him wherever he went. She was only one little fish, outclassed in a shoal of celebrities.

Alessandro held all the cards in life—breeding, money and confidence—while she had none. The sad thing was, he hardly seemed to enjoy any of them.

CHAPTER NINE

MICHELLE regarded him as she took a sip of her drink. 'You really know how to live, Alessandro,' she said, placing the glass down carefully beside her plate.

His eyes were veiled, and he didn't reply. She had so many questions to ask him. Feeling rested and fortified by the wonderful food, she could not resist working her way towards the one that burned most insistently in her mind.

'All this beauty encased by such a hi-tech security system.' She gazed at the banks of pastel-pink cyclamen and trailing ferns ranged around them. Jasmine twining in and out of citrus and mimosa bushes added to the feeling of sitting in a beautiful garden. 'How many people have made it through your defences?' she whispered.

'None so far.' His voice was a low growl, snatching back her attention.

It was the opening she needed. 'Then it's all the more amazing that you called me your fiancée in front of that press pack.'

'I've told you. It's the easiest solution. We'll get married as soon as possible to legitimise the baby. That way

I satisfy my conscience, the House of Castiglione gets the heir it needs, and I don't have to worry about adverse publicity any more. Things will improve still further when the baby arrives. We'll project the perfect image of family life.'

He outlined his plans with ease. Michelle could hardly believe what she was hearing. 'You're going to use our baby as a photo opportunity?'

He gave a leonine smile. 'No. In a refreshing break with recent Castiglione tradition, I'm going to be fiercely protective of my child. No offspring of mine will ever be used to get cheap publicity. Neither will it be used as a pawn, currency or its mother's latest fashion accessory.'

Momentarily thrown off balance, Michelle reacted by trying to laugh. 'You sound like a press release, Alessandro!'

He inclined his head gravely. 'I'm a realist. That's why I warned you not to be tempted to fall in love with me.'

Michelle had felt a million things for him over the past few months, although love wasn't quite the right word for any of them. Lust and longing, certainly, but love? She wasn't actually sure what that was. With no experience of how it felt to love and be loved in return, how could she possibly know?

Looking at this charismatic and awe-inspiring man, she felt a new ambition begin to steal over her. She knew what it was like to live within an isolation tank of work and duty. Breaking down the barriers that surrounded Alessandro would be a real achievement. It was something that would do them *both* good. And, she reminded herself, there were worse things in life than moving into the guest wing of a Tuscan villa. Unemployed single parenthood back in England, for one.

Smiling up at him mischeviously from beneath her lashes, she tried to find some chink in his armour. 'Didn't it ever occur to you that I'd taken you at your word, Alessandro? That I might have grown to hate you for abandoning me, and that I might refuse your offer to move in here?'

Her words only proved to Alessandro how inexperienced she really was.

'No, it didn't—not for a second. I saw you needed help. I'm the one to give it, however it might make me feel. There was no way you could turn me down.' He shook his head. 'Are you ready for dessert?'

He looked pointedly at her meal. Michelle had been so wrapped up in her thoughts about him that she had abandoned it. Not wanting to keep him waiting, she nodded. To speak might have broken the spell she was beginning to weave for herself. In her mind she had already started to chip away at his icy reserve.

A maid appeared from nowhere and placed a magnificent gateau in the centre of the table.

'The French call this *nid d'abeilles*.' Alessandro picked up a silver cake slice. 'Would you like some?'

The cake was a cloud of featherlight brioche, filled with *crème anglaise*. Michelle admired the glistening confection with its topping of toasted almonds.

'I can't say no to something so tempting.' Michelle looked up, and when she saw the glimmer in his eyes her cheeks pinkened and she looked away, embarrassed.

But a teasing smile haunted his lips as he watched her

reaction, and slowly it fuelled Michelle's budding arousal until she ached for him in a way she had never experienced before. She knew it was wicked, but now she had seen him smile she needed more. She wanted his touch.

Alessandro cut her a portion of gateau. Lifting it onto a delicate bone china plate, he passed it to her. She wished there could be another excuse for their hands to touch as it passed between them, but it wasn't to be. The half-smile in Alessandro's eyes almost made up for it—but not quite. Even so, for a moment she persuaded herself those blinds obscuring his true feelings had allowed a sliver of encouragement to escape. Colouring, she looked down and reached for her cutlery.

'Wait—don't start yet. There's an important finishing touch.'

The maid materialised at his elbow with a cut-glass jar of honey.

'Won't that make this cake too sweet?' Michelle frowned as Alessandro offered it to her.

'My chef uses less sugar in the recipe. Honey is the ideal accompaniment. It's produced on the Villa Castiglione estate.'

With his encouragement, Michelle leaned forward to breathe in the honey's distinctive fragrance. It was heavy with the perfume of flowers.

'Try it.'

She was hesitant, having tried supermarket honey once without liking it. Only Alessandro's persuasive powers made her pick up the intricately cast silver honey server. She twirled it in the jar of bottled sunshine. Trailing glossy liquid over her dessert, she smiled.

'This isn't a bit like the stuff I've had in the past.'

'Would you like more?' His accent turned the words into a purr.

'Oh, yes…' Michelle breathed, in a way that had nothing whatever to do with honey.

There was a pause as he looked at her plate and raised his dark brows.

'But you haven't tried it yet.' Putting the honey jar back on its silver salver, he positioned it between them on the table. 'Later, perhaps?'

Beneath the table, his knee brushed against hers. Light-headed with longing, Michelle hoped it wasn't an accident. She gripped her spoon and fork tightly, concentrating on carving out a little taste of the gateau.

Any worries she had about not liking the *nid d'abeilles* dissolved instantly. Its combination of tastes and textures was a divine marriage. She closed her eyes and enjoyed.

'Quite an experience, isn't it?' Alessandro's voice strolled through her soul.

'It's wonderful.'

She finished the whole slice, right down to the last smudge of honey on her plate. Then she sat back with a sigh.

'Every bit of that was absolutely delicious.'

'I'm glad you enjoyed it.' He had already finished his own dessert, and was watching her over steepled fingers. 'Would you like coffee?'

'I'd better not,' Michelle said with real regret. She would have jumped at any excuse to carry on sitting so close to Alessandro—except that one. 'I haven't been able to stand the smell of it since—'

'I can imagine.' Alessandro cut across her words

before she could mention her pregnancy. 'They say it affects every part of your life.'

She nodded, conscious that he must want to skirt around the issue. Powerful feelings were torturing her. They had nothing to do with pregnancy but everything to do with Alessandro.

'And mine...' He stood up, the delicate legs of his chair rattling against the stone tiles of the conservatory floor. 'Would you like a tour of your new home? If you're not too tired,' he added as an afterthought.

The thought of being squired around a Tuscan villa at dusk was wonderful. The fact her guide would be none other than Alessandro took a little getting used to. After an uncertain start, today had been a dream spun from fantasies. She had been whisked into a completely different world. There was so much to take in, and despite Alessandro's simmering resentment, Michelle couldn't resist the chance to spend more time with him. Perhaps she would wake up and find it had all been some kind of feverish delusion. Everything might disappear in a puff of reality. It could happen. After all, Alessandro had vanished from her life once already, taking her happiness with him. What was to stop him doing the same thing again?

She set off on his guided tour determined not to be over-awed. It was impossible. There was so much to take in. The moment he led her down to the custom built spa, her mouth dropped open. The best she could hope for after that was to try and hide her wonderment. It was difficult. The changing rooms alone were larger than her cottage back in England. When Alessandro led her through to the pool and bar, she walked into heaven.

'You should take plenty of exercise. I've checked, and swimming is something you can enjoy right up to the time the baby is born,' he said with satisfaction.

Michelle gazed at the tasteful mosaics of fruit and flowers on the tiled floor and walls of the pool. They glowed with colour from underwater lighting.

'All the steamer chairs are inside today. Normally they are outside on the terrace, taking advantage of the view.' He pointed across the huge room to the far wall, which was completely glazed.

'It's like a tropical garden!' Michelle looked around at the huge terracotta planters standing in every corner and around the bar. They billowed with all sorts of exotic foliage. Palms, bananas and marantas revelled in the warm, humid atmosphere. She went over to admire a fountain of orchid blossoms, and was amazed to see a pretty little tree frog blinking at her from among the leaves.

'The original pair arrived hidden among some imported plants. They love it here, and have bred happily ever since,' Alessandro said softly from somewhere just behind her.

Michelle hadn't realised he had followed her so closely. She spun round on her heel, and saw his expression slip from amusement to gravity.

'I'm happy to let them stay—as long as they behave themselves.'

She raised her eyebrows, wondering if the same rules applied to her. If Alessandro monitored the behaviour of wild creatures so carefully, he might intend doing the same to her.

Alessandro inspired such conflicting feelings. From the moment she'd set eyes on him she'd known no other man would ever exist for her. His unexplained disappearance from the villa Jolie Fleur had almost destroyed her. Her self-esteem had been totally wrecked. When she'd discovered she was carrying his child, it might have been a disaster too far. Instead, it had proved to be an unlikely lifeline. Preparing to try and give her child the sort of life she'd been denied had kept Michelle going through those dark, early days of depression. That was why she had to fall in with Alessandro's plans now. However bizarre his actions in bringing her here and arranging a loveless marriage, it would at least give her baby the chance of a perfect childhood.

And it might eventually give me some hope of happiness for myself, she thought, daring to slide a sideways glance at Alessandro as he led her through his vast ancestral home. Until they'd met she had spent every one of her twenty-three years worrying what other people thought of her. Then, for a few glorious summer days, Alessandro had blown all her fears away. He filled her mind and senses until nothing else had mattered. However much she tried to recall the angry side of him, she was fighting a swelling tide of much happier memories. She feasted her eyes on him whenever she thought it was safe to do so. Alessandro's cool, aristocratic presence set her senses dancing. And, to judge by his expression, he was fighting to restrain his own impulses, too.

It wasn't long before Michelle discovered what they were. As dusk crept up from the shadows of the ancient building, their leisurely ramble around the Villa Castiglione reached the great entrance hall on the ground floor.

'This is where I arrived earlier. It must mean the end

of my tour,' she said with real regret. She was trying to avoid looking towards his office. That was a place of painful embarrassment for her. She went all hot and cold at the thought of throwing up not once, but twice in front of him.

Alessandro had no such qualms. He was heading over to the white painted door, and when he reached it, looked back at her expectantly. 'You still have the master suite to see.'

He pushed open the door and leaned back against it. There was no escape. Michelle had to walk past him, into the heart of his house.

Alessandro's office was full of the warm, stuffy smell of top-quality paper and brand-new fittings. Without the demon sickness pulling her towards his executive bathroom, Michelle had time to appreciate the pot plants spilling flowers and foliage from every nook. He led her out to the executive lift that would take them right to the top of the building again. When its mirrored doors slid open they were in a world where sound was softened by thick cream carpet and the exotic foliage of planted arrangements. Like the villa's spa area, palm fronds and sprays of orchids were everywhere. They swayed seductively in warm, filtered air. But when they reached Alessandro's suite of rooms, she heard the sound of birdsong.

'Oh, an aviary!' she gasped, seeing tropical birds flitting among the leaves in one protected corner. 'I've always wanted one of those!'

He made a wry face and followed her over to the gilded wire of an enormous enclosure filling one end of the lobby. The birds initially took fright at the sight of

Michelle, but when they recognised Alessandro they hopped out into view again.

'Really? *Dio*, it's the last thing I'd wish for.' He marvelled at her. 'It's always been here. My father never believed in leaving anything to chance. Anything he might want to do or see, like birds, had to be on the spot. I don't approve of caging anything, but these little creatures get the very best care around the clock. I wouldn't feel happy entrusting them to anyone else, so they'll have a home here for the rest of their natural lives. But when they die I'll never replace them. Poor things.'

He gave them a smile that touched Michelle's heart.

'But come on—it's getting late. You can visit them again after you've seen the rest of my suite.'

Michelle looked dubiously towards a pair of cream doors leading from the lobby. The clean smell of fresh paint sharpened her senses. Although she wanted to break down Alessandro's distrust of her, this felt like an intrusion too far.

'I'm not sure…we hardly know each other…'

'You are the mother of my child, and I've introduced you everywhere today as my fiancée. There can't be anyone better qualified to judge the redecorations that have been done for me.'

He ushered her through the doors into a large drawing room beyond the lobby. Cool and sophisticated, in pale green and cream, it was made still more beautiful by the accent of dark rugs and tasteful arrangements of antiques and artwork. Alcoves around the walls displayed discreetly lit expensive crystal. Michelle could not stop staring. Lovely things kept catching her eye, but Alessandro didn't give his surroundings a second glance. He led her straight through a pair of tall French doors and onto a balcony.

A delicate tracery of railings was the only thing that stood between them and the Castiglione estate. Although darkness was falling fast, Michelle had a sense of great space, contained only by the bulk of hills that rose up all around Alessandro's ancestral lands. A distant twinkle of lights showed where the road threaded its way along the Tiebolino valley. Now and then the shape of an owl broke away from the shelter of the chestnut trees. The sound of its call echoed like mournful music through the countryside.

'I can waste minutes on end out here,' Alessandro said in a confiding tone she hadn't heard for weeks. 'The whole place is usually deserted by the time I'm free to go on the prowl. But occasionally someone's life comes into my field of vision for a few moments—a member of my indoor staff, or one of the estate workers. I might overhear a few words, or witness a scene—then they're gone. What happens after that is none of my business, only theirs—unless it requires money, of course.' His expression hardened, and she saw his hands clench on the balcony rail. 'Then I'm the first port of call for everyone.'

Despite the jaded tone he used to talk about cash, there was a certain satisfaction in his voice. Michelle was intrigued. She had never known anyone who enjoyed observing others from a distance in the same way she did. Until he'd said that she had assumed his life as an international tycoon was filled with other people's lives.

'It's perfect, isn't it?' She smiled, relaxing a little. 'For a while you can enjoy a kind of intimacy with others, but they can't expect anything from you. They don't know you exist. Watching from up here must give you the perfect camouflage. I wish I'd had somewhere like this back home in England.'

'Why would you need to hide?' he asked unexpectedly.

'Oh, I've always been much happier to melt into the background.'

It was a few seconds before Alessandro replied. His answer was filled with the bitter tang of experience. 'At least you've had a choice.'

Michelle laughed out loud at that.

'You must be joking! My mother entered me for the Miss Bubbles competition every year from the age of one.'

'Miss Bubbles?' Alessandro's beautiful dark eyes were puzzled.

'It's a nationwide beauty pageant sponsored by a British soap manufacturer,' Michelle explained. 'The winner gets her picture on the pack for a year, and their own weight in each one of the company's dozens of products.'

Alessandro tried to look impressed. It was no good. For once Michelle could see right through him. She knew he was laughing at her secretly. Everyone always had—especially the judges.

'Did you win?'

'Not once—in five attempts. My mum spent a fortune on hairspray and elocution lessons for me, but it was no good. She was always disappointed. Right from the moment I was born. She wanted a doll to dress up, but instead she got—me.' Michelle spread her hands wide in a hopeless gesture.

Alessandro gave a hollow laugh. 'I think that is called in English fishing for compliments?'

The look on Michelle's face when he said that brought out the cynic in him.

'Oh, come on! You're breaking my heart, Michelle. Surely it wasn't so bad, being pampered and groomed all the time?'

Instead, she shook her head. 'Exhibiting me was Mum's hobby,' she said simply. 'Much later, when Dad died and Mum was left with no money coming into the house, she realised what my teachers had been saying all along. I'm just not size-zero material and I never have been. We had to find work, and beyond art I wasn't qualified to do anything beyond cleaning.'

'So you had to give up the spotlight?'

'It was a relief! I spent all my time trying to back out of its glare,' Michelle said ruefully. 'And "the older they get, the cuter they ain't," as my dear old mum used to say!'

She laughed, but Alessandro's smile quickly faded into something far more serious.

'Not so. You look cute enough to me.' Slowly, his hand slid along the wrought-iron balustrade. He needed to say something to bridge the gap between them, but English was too revealing. '*Li ho mancati*, Michelle.'

To soften his gruff confession he reached out to touch her arm. As she turned towards him it fell away, like gossamer evaporating in sunlight.

'I don't speak Italian,' Michelle reminded him. 'You said you were going to find me a tutor.'

Laughter came, thick in his throat. 'Of course—how could I forget?'

'So? What were you saying?'

He shrugged. 'I'm not in the habit of repeating my-self. The faster you learn my language the better. When

I'm at the villa I don't have enough time to waste in translation. I've got better things to do, and other people to speak with.'

Michelle felt his words like a blow. For the first time the reality of a marriage of convenience with Alessandro struck home. He would be calling the shots. Her future would consist of long periods abandoned here at the villa, Alessandro's secrets, and probably more lies.

It did not seem to occur to him that this was more honesty than Michelle wanted. His eyes were as dark as memory, but despite that laughter still danced in them. Michelle was hurting, but she had to hide her pain. She tried to laugh, but it was impossible. All she managed was a smile. His hand returned to her arm and he guided her back into his suite. His movements had a fluidity that distracted her from further questions.

'Come—you only have one room left to see. The place closest to every Italian man's heart—his kitchen.'

The kitchen of Alessandro's suite was as glossy and well equipped as the rest of his home. Michelle took a moment to marvel before noticing something. More than any other room in his beautiful home, this one was totally unnatural. The showroom condition of the glossy cherrywood cabinets was just *too* perfect. Every surface was spotless. The place was totally devoid of any human touch. There were no pot plants, biscuit tins, fridge magnets or noticeboards.

It was chilling. She had been shown the villa's enormous kitchens downstairs, and Alessandro had live-in staff to keep the place clean. That would explain why this part of his suite looked unused, but she suspected it hid a deeper truth. The thing Michelle found scary was that, in common with the rest of his villa, Alessandro's kitchen had no heart.

The last rays of sun vanished as they completed the grand tour. Wearily, Michelle followed Alessandro back into his reception room. Reaching some switches on the wall, he pressed them. Discreet lamps instantly shed soft light around the newly decorated room, but the contrast of light and shade made her feel momentarily dizzy.

Sensing something wasn't quite right, Alessandro went straight back to where she was standing. She had one hand pressed to her brow. Looking into her face, he frowned. 'You're exhausted,' he said softly.

'I'm fine. It's nothing but a dizzy spell. They pass.'

'But what about the baby?'

There was a tinge of reproof in his voice. Michelle bit her lip. She had got so used to pushing herself through all the weary, lonely days of her pregnancy so far. It must be difficult for an outsider, especially a privileged one like Alessandro, to understand how 'the show must go on'.

'It isn't an illness, Alessandro. The doctor says I should carry on as normal.'

He was unimpressed. 'That's *your* doctor's opinion, maybe, but you must be guided by *my* doctor from now on. He's calling first thing tomorrow to check you over.' He clicked his tongue and frowned. 'Are you sure you're OK? Your guest suite is right on the farthest side of the villa. It's quite a walk back.'

'I'll be fine. All I need is a few minutes' rest and a drink, if you have one.'

'Of course.'

He guided her across the room to one of several soft

easy chairs drawn up around a big old fireplace. Settling
her there with a look of grave concern, he turned his attention to the grate. A neat arrangement of sticks and
crumpled newspaper lay in it, ready for use.

'If you can't drink coffee, what can you tolerate?' he
asked, kneeling down to light the fire. Any time Michelle
tried to do such a thing it inevitably led to messy hands
and failure. When Alessandro struck a match, flames
leapt into life instantly beneath his fingers, as she had
known they would.

'Another glass of still mineral water would be fine.'

Alessandro sat back on his heels and snorted dismis-
sively. 'Do you not want something warm when there's
such a chill in the air?'

Michelle had the perfect answer to that. 'I could never
find decent tea when I was in France during the summer.'

'Ah, but now you're at the Villa Castiglione.'

Brushing off his hands, Alessandro stood up to admire the blaze he had kindled. 'I got a taste for tea when
I was sent away to boarding school in England. I had
to—it was either that or stay thirsty. The kitchens here
always have a good supply of anything my guests might
want. What blend do you drink?'

Michelle was tired and overwrought, but couldn't
help laughing at his concern. 'Does your kitchen stock
supermarket special?'

'Now, that's something I *can't* offer you.' His face
softened with a smile, thawed by the fire and the warm-
ing atmosphere. 'Your choices begin with Indian or
China, and get more exotic and complicated from then
on. So—what do you fancy?'

'I have absolutely no idea.' Michelle began to feel

better. She giggled, spreading her hands wide and letting them fall on the arms of her chair.

After that soft sound there was an instant of perfect silence. It was broken only by the crackle of logs on the fire. In that moment she realised exactly what she wanted. And, to judge by the fleeting look in his eyes, so did Alessandro.

'When it comes to tea, I'll let you decide for me,' she said quietly.

He nodded. There was a moment's hesitation—and then he walked over to a telephone hidden away on the window seat.

Only minutes after his whispered conversation with the kitchens, a tray of drinks and more food was delivered.

'Your people feed you so much!' Michelle observed as soon as they were alone again.

'They try, but I prefer quality to quantity,' he said, pouring a cup of tea and handing it to her.

It's little considerations like this that set him apart, Michelle thought as she accepted it. The Royal Worcester cup chimed prettily as she stirred in some milk with a solid silver teaspoon. As she looked at the small display of *petit fours* and miniature *biscotti* laid out for them, the delicious meal she had eaten seemed long ago and far away.

'Go ahead.' He smiled, fixing himself a drink from the tray. 'Don't be shy.'

She chose a perfect triangle of lemon sponge, hardly bigger than her thumbnail, and then a tiny almond *tuile*.

'Have some more,' he coaxed. 'It's all there to be eaten.'

'Oh, but it's such a wicked selection…' she said with real longing, looking at a miniature meringue that was hardly big enough to contain the wild strawberry nestling within its curls.

'I insist that all the ingredients come from my estates,' Alessandro said with satisfaction. 'That way, every mouthful is guaranteed to do you good.'

'I'm sure it will,' Michelle said with relish, and didn't need a second invitation to treat herself.

Five minutes later they had finished everything, and Michelle's eyelids were drooping in the warm, dusky comfort of her armchair.

'You're looking better already,' Alessandro said with quiet satisfaction.

His words jerked her awake. She sat up quickly. He was standing beside her, and raised a hand in warning.

'Take it easy—there's no rush. Would you like another cup of tea?'

'Yes—yes, please.' Michelle automatically reached for the teapot at exactly the same time Alessandro did.

In the soft light of evening his fingers closed over hers—at first by accident, then with a definite pressure. It could mean only one thing, but Michelle was afraid her slightest movement might fracture the fantasy. They were both trying to do the same thing at the same time, so it might have been an accident. But then he bent forward to rest his head lightly against hers...

The impulses Michelle had been suppressing all day pushed her gently into the warm solidity of him. In one movement he drew her hand back from the tea tray and enfolded her in his arms. When he touched her cheek, it freed all her pent-up passion at last. Twisting in his grasp to face him, she accepted his kisses with a hunger beyond caring.

CHAPTER TEN

PLEASURE had been the only thing on Alessandro's mind that morning. The news of Michelle's pregnancy had crushed that, consuming his brain with the need to legitimise his child. That was his duty. So where was the pleasure in that?

The answer was Michelle. The curve of her cheek, the gentle flow of her hair—everything about her was crying out for his touch. When she had crumpled into this chair, so vulnerable and pale, Alessandro had known the time for self-control had come to an end. Gathering her up like this and inspiring her with new life was the most natural thing in the world.

He tried to make his kisses slow and leisurely, but his desire for her had been caged for months. It could barely be contained. Her body was trembling beneath his touch. It had been so long—far too long. He felt her desire burning within the thin cotton of her top. It was wonderful. He covered her face in kisses, teasing moans of pleasure from her as she closed her eyes, full of the aching delight of it all. As her fingers kneaded his shoulders he found her mouth again and kissed her quivering lips.

The soaring power of her response acted on Alessandro

like the most powerful aphrodisiac, but it couldn't stop his mind working. That was the trouble with being a 'face' on the international stage. It made you unnaturally wary. Each time someone smiled or tried to be friendly Alessandro got suspicious. He had the example of his parents to blame for that. Too often in the past people had approached him only in the hope of getting their picture in the paper, or worse. So far Alessandro had outmanoeuvred every plan. He had managed to repair the damage done to the House of Castiglione's image by his mother, father and his warring relatives. Michelle was not going to be allowed to jeopardise his peace of mind. He wasn't going to let her get inside his mind.

He'd have her—but on his own terms. Marrying her would secure his heir. It would also give him every legal opportunity to indulge in sex with her without any emotional entanglement. Romance was for single people. Sex was for grown-ups, like them.

He smiled as his kisses and caresses drew her smoothly towards an absolutely stellar experience. Whispering encouragement, sometimes in the music of his own language, sometimes with the sweetest words she had ever heard, he placed kisses all over her cheeks, lips and forehead. As the tip of his tongue danced around her ear, he murmured, 'Have I ever told you my eyes couldn't get enough of you, from the first moment I stepped off that helicopter?'

'Never. Tell me now…' It was the voice of a husky stranger. Michelle could hardly believe the words had come from her own lips, and giggled.

Alessandro felt his body rise in anticipation. Her voice was a low, throaty chuckle, and it was all woman.

She was his. There could be no doubt about it. For a few glorious moments he allowed himself to focus totally on the sensations rippling through his muscular body. Nothing else mattered for him. Their past and future were irrelevant. Only the present consumed him.

The thought of it ran kisses of fire over his skin as he caressed the inviting curves of her body. Michelle warmed beneath his hands, flowing like honey and equally sweet to the taste. The closer he got to her, the more difficult it was to focus on one single charm. Even the nervous tension that tortured her every moment had a strange fascination for him. He could feel it now, expressed in the taut line of her throat. Pausing, he reassured her softly.

She could hear him whispering, but barely registered what he was saying. It was impossible not to return his kisses, but her muscles were beginning to bunch for flight. Breaking free from his mouth, she managed to gasp, 'You're nothing like the Alessandro I used to know.'

'Aren't I?' He chuckled, deep into the side of her neck. 'But you're *exactly* as I remember you!'

It's not true, he thought. *Back in the summer she was as willing as water. Today—today I cannot tell which woman she is. One always looking out for the next opportunity to fleece a man, or the innocent I had in my bed?*

He knew how Michelle worked, and she'd never be able to wrong-foot him again. Tonight he planned to take what she offered, but it wouldn't make any difference to her future. He'd marry her, ensuring his child could be kept safe at the villa, but otherwise she wouldn't be allowed to affect his life in any way. Like all women, she would soon tire of his work ethic and find other ways to amuse herself. He intended to be the perfect father, providing everything his child could ever need or want. What Michelle chose to do would be absolutely no concern of his—as long as she behaved like the perfect mother in public.

His own mother had strayed in public, but unlike his father, Alessandro was determined not to react by conducting his own affairs across the pages of glossy magazines. He was going to control everything the world learned about his family, no matter how much it cost and whatever the private sacrifice. The future was about this baby, not his feelings. Alessandro's priorities were to give his child a proper upbringing right from the start, and make it a legitimate heir for the family firm. Nothing else mattered.

But at times, in Michelle's looks, her sighs, her words, he thought he saw more in her—the woman he'd once thought she was. But it was dangerous to give that thought free rein.

Michelle's perfume drifted around him on the warm air, bringing him back to the present.

'Alessandro,' she murmured.

Something was definitely happening to him. He could feel it in the way his shoulders were loosening up. And he found he was appreciating all those little details that set Michelle apart from his usual quarry. Her soft, curvaceous beauty felt wonderful beneath his fingers. The feel of her, and those deliciously shy smiles she gave him, stood out in stark contrast to the bony triumph and niggling demands of the women who usually came looking for his attention.

'I don't do fidelity,' he reminded himself aloud, just

so she could be under no illusion. 'I told you as much in the summer.'

He had to say it, to stop her getting too close. Alessandro had his suspicions that she was cast in the same mould as his parents. She had hidden the truth from him once before, during those lazy days in the South of France. All the time her apparent expertise and smiles had told him one thing, when the reality had been quite different…

For a split second the memory of taking her virginity acted on Alessandro like a slap in the face. He hesitated, but quickly hardened his heart. Yes, he'd left her while she slept, but he had only done it to secure her future. He'd only wanted a fling, and staying any longer would only have meant putting off the moment when he broke her heart. He had thought his way would be kinder, and he had done his best to make amends.

Knowing her dream of an idyllic cottage and a chance to work with the art she loved, he had arranged it all through his charitable foundation. When she had never bothered to contact him on the number he had put in his letter of goodbye, he had assumed she wanted to forget the whole affair.

In his eyes, there was nothing to be guilty about now. Marrying her would seal the deal. It would stop her trying to cash in on his child by using the poor little mite as a bargaining tool. And marriage would give Michelle the satisfaction of a regular income for life—as long as she played by his rules. In Alessandro's experience, money was the worm at the core of every apple. This way, he got to control exactly where it went…

He sampled Michelle's full, rose-pink lips again. Her deliciousness soon pushed every reproach from his mind. All day her subtle beauty had tempted him with glimpses of what the future held. Now he was going to rediscover the charms of her body as though it was the first time.

'You want me. You've always wanted me. Let me take you now,' he growled.

It was a bold statement, but despite his powerful urge to ravish her right there in the firelight, Alessandro wanted this decision to be hers. He had been too impetuous the first time. When she tensed beneath his fingers he guessed what it meant. He stiffened, silently compelling her to change her mind.

'We both know how good it is between us.' His voice was husky and full of longing.

In contrast, Michelle's reply was clipped and desperate. She peeled herself away from him and looked up into his face. Her expression was searching. 'I can't. We mustn't. I was too carried away to call a halt that evening in the villa, but I have to make a stand tonight, Alessandro. You have to realise I'm not the woman you thought I was. That's why I can't give in to you again before our wedding. It's not in my nature.' Her eyes became hooded in a way that unsettled him. 'If you *really* intend marrying me, you won't mind.'

Alessandro pulled back sharply. With a gasp of disbelief he let her go, and ran a hand irritably through his hair.

'I've spent a long time living down my father's bad reputation. I'd *never* have brought you here for anything less than marriage. Of course I'm going to marry you. What do you think I am?' His voice was dark.

Her reply was instant. 'The sort of man who took my virginity and left me to wake up alone?'

'I did what I thought was the best thing at the time. Was it my fault if you gave up at the first attempt at getting through on my private line?'

'I was ashamed and embarrassed for being so weak-willed and sleeping with you, Alessandro. Ashamed because I'd always intended to be a virgin on my wedding day—and embarrassed because…' She looked down at the floor quickly, blushing as all those conflicting feelings came rushing back. 'Because I enjoyed it. If I *had* found you again the next day, I'm not sure I could have looked you in the eyes…'

Slowly, gradually, his expression warmed, until the hint of a smile parted his lips. 'You've been managing quite well today.'

She looked up, and they exchanged the flash of a quick smile.

'We're in an unusual situation, aren't we? Perhaps… well, perhaps there were faults on both sides,' he continued with difficulty, adding quickly, 'Don't be too hard on yourself, *carina.*'

Closing the gap between them again, he placed a delicate kiss on the tip of her nose. Cupping her head in one of his warm brown hands, he burnished the gleam of her hair. 'We've both been having a rough time, but that's all behind us now. I told you back in the summer—it's OK to enjoy life, Michelle. Relax, and give yourself the chance to live.'

Tentatively, she returned his smile. When she leaned against his touch this time, Alessandro bent his head and dropped a tingle of exquisite kisses over the thin skin of her throat. It silenced Michelle, but couldn't calm her mind. She had always thought she was less than human, because for her, enjoying life seemed impossible. Guilt was everywhere, and never more painful than today. She was pregnant, and desperate enough to believe the promises of a man who'd already abandoned her once.

What would Mum have said? The thought tortured her. It tried to push her out of Alessandro's arms. But she could hardly tell him that.

Suddenly she realised she couldn't tell him anything at all. He was filling her senses to the exclusion of everything else. All her worries evaporated as he nuzzled her breast through the thin cotton of her top. With a gasp her head fell back, and she revelled in the deliciously sensual feeling of his lips pressing the fabric against her aroused nipples. Unless she stopped him right now, she would be lost all over again.

'Michelle…' His warm breath whispered through to her skin. 'There's no need for you to deny yourself any more… Unless you really, honestly want to…'

It was the chance of a lifetime. Michelle thought back to their days beneath the summer sun. The experience was still so sweet in her memory. What was to stop her enjoying it all over again? And this time would be even better. She would be Alessandro's wife, living right here at the hub of everything that meant anything to him. If she was accepted into his home she could try to work her way into his life. She could start by trying to grab back the brief happiness they had shared in summer with both hands—

Cold, hard reality trampled that fantasy underfoot. Alessandro was offering her an all-expenses-paid life in return for a share in their child. That was all—no promises of love or romance. She would be reduced to living off him. Life alone in England had been hard, but Michelle had been discovering her independence and making it work. Now Alessandro had taken complete charge of where she would be living and what she would eat. She began to panic. She would lose everything, and be absorbed by him. She would be totally dependent on him for everything.

Alessandro was caressing her in a way he knew she couldn't resist. In desperation, Michelle knew she had to stop him before her body bypassed her mind and started giving the orders.

'No—stop, Alessandro. I can't.'

Digging her fingers into the curve of his back, she pushed him away. It was a rougher action than she'd intended, but she had to be harsh. Betraying her feelings would give him too much leverage over her emotions.

'I can't marry without love, Alessandro.'

'Why not?'

He stopped and gazed at her, nonplussed.

'Because it wouldn't be right!' she said, amazed he could be so cavalier about something so important.

'Rubbish! It is the only option. It will legitimise our baby, secure the future of the company and make sure this lovely old house carries my family's name into the next generation.'

Michelle looked at him with new eyes. Despite her past experience of him, there was no doubting his sincerity about this. Tradition was so important to him, and she knew his pride would be her downfall. If she refused to marry him he would sever all connection with her for ever.

She thought of her poor, innocent little baby, cast adrift because of her scruples, and came to a decision.

'I suppose the Castigliones have been doing this sort of thing for centuries?' she said slowly. 'Choosing a wife for hard-headed, practical reasons rather than love?'

Alessandro nodded with satisfaction. '*Certo*. Can you think of a more logical thing to do? You'll live here as my wife, and supervise the upbringing of my children. Everyone will be happy.'

Something about his bold assertion made her wonder.

'So…you're planning on having more children?' She stroked her tummy thoughtfully. 'I'm still coming to terms with carrying this one.'

'Don't worry—you won't necessarily have to *do* anything. That's what staff are for,' Alessandro murmured. 'It's your presence in the Villa Castiglione that is important. You'll be the heart of my home. I want you on call twenty-four hours a day, every day.'

'And what will you be doing while I'm being Queen Bee of the nursery?'

He stared down at her as though it might be a trick question.

'I'll be at work, of course. I've already told you I don't spend much time here.'

'And you'll be in the Florence office?' she ventured hopefully.

He looked puzzled. 'Possibly…sometimes. I travel all over the world. Wherever the House of Castiglione wants me, that's where I'm based.'

'But…not always here at home?'

He frowned at her continual probing.

'Hardly ever.' He shrugged. 'That's the way these relationships work. Distance can often make them stronger.'

'Can it? Who told you that?'

His eyes evaded hers. 'Oh, I must have picked the saying up from somewhere.'

'A child needs two parents.' Michelle sent his own words spinning back to him.

'Yes—one to work, and one to care.'

'I'd rather we both cared for our child—together.'

'Neither of you will ever want for anything.' His intensity was completely convincing. Michelle would have nodded, but she still needed to make a point.

'I'm not interested in money or things. You can keep it all, Alessandro, as long as I can keep my baby,' she said simply.

He dipped his head. 'Thank you for being so reasonable.'

That brought a smile to her lips. 'I don't feel reasonable. I feel ungainly and uncomfortable.' She looked down at her damp pink palms and sighed. Making a move to rub them over her jeans, she remembered where she was just in time and stopped. The corner of an immaculately pressed handkerchief flipped into her field of view. With a sigh she took it, glancing up at Alessandro as she did so. There was a fragile smile on his lips.

'As far as I'm concerned you look radiant,' he said softly.

'I must look hot, bothered, and the worst possible advertisement for pregnancy,' she persisted.

But Alessandro had no time for her self-pity. His body swayed closer, touching hers. One hand cupped her shoulder. The other pressed an index finger gently against her lips.

'You're talking like a risk-assessor, *carissima*. Stop it—and fly.'

She closed her eyes, remembering their first and last carefree coupling. But there was a direct route from that indescribable happiness to Alessandro's coldly efficient marriage proposal. She had given her all to this vibrant, sexy man, and seen him reduce her dreams to a cost-benefit analysis. Now he was turning the charm on again. It was so *very* tempting…

'Oh, how I wish I thought I could trust you, Alessandro.'

'A Castiglione never breaks his word,' he said quietly. 'I will care for you for as long as you are the mother of my child.'

The thought of what he had been to her in the past pressed Michelle on. She wanted to experience that special fulfilment only Alessandro could bring her. Surely the life sentence of being his wife in nothing but name was worth it for the chance to soar with him once again?

Or twice…? Or maybe more times…?

He had suggested there would be more children…

Michelle came to a decision. If that was what it took to stay within Alessandro's orbit, then she would do it. If she went back to England she might never see him again. At least he said he visited the Villa Castiglione from time to time. That was something.

'Then, yes…I'll marry you, Alessandro.' She ducked her head, anticipating a guffaw of relief, laughter—in fact, anything rather than what actually happened, which was silence. After a pause, she heard him draw in a staccato breath.

'I'll make sure you never regret it, Michelle,' he murmured in one single exhalation. 'Let me show you…'

His arms fastened more tightly around her. *We fit so exactly. It's as if our bodies were made for each other*, she thought. *We're in one mind about the baby too, but beyond that, what have we got?* She drew back a minute distance, wondering if she had the strength of will to resist him. *Can my physical need for him make up for the bad times?* she thought. *When I don't know where he is, but I can guess what he's doing?*

The answer came back: *I don't know.*

'I may not offer you love, Michelle, but at least I'm being honest about it,' he murmured into her ear. 'We're both adults. I need you, you need me. And the baby comes before us both. This will be a perfect arrangement. We'll all get everything we could possibly desire. You'll live a life of luxury here, and the baby will always have first call on my time. Any time, anywhere, my heir takes precedence. I'll be here,' he finished, so emphatically that she believed him.

It was a turning point. Until then Alessandro had only seduced her through her dreams. Now it was happening for real. He was kissing her and caressing her and driving her out of her mind with longing. Despite and because of everything that had happened between them, Michelle could not resist. All sorts of alarms rang in her head, but they were muffled. She could think of nothing more than the pleasure of being in his arms and under his spell.

She gazed up at him, knowing that a man like this

could never confine himself within the arms of one woman. She knew she was setting herself up for heartbreak all over again. *But then*, she reminded herself, *I'm used to that.* At least she could grab these minutes, maybe even a few hours of pleasure, before grim reality kicked in again. For now, for once, it was enough to relish every second she could, enjoying Alessandro while her feelings for him were still free of any regrets.

When he asked her again, there was only one possible answer she could give him. With a sad, sweet smile she told him breathlessly, 'Yes…take me again, Alessandro. Please…like the first time.'

CHAPTER ELEVEN

HER words brought Alessandro's body to boiling point again. He caught her hand, ready to lead her towards his bedroom, but lust overcame him. He stopped and took her face between his hands. Then he kissed her, long and hard. As his hands slipped down to roam over her body, his tongue probed the intimacy of her mouth with a precision that took her breath away.

Between kisses he murmured, 'I'm all yours. Undress for me.'

Unconsciously, Michelle drew back. Alessandro frowned. He tried to question her eyes, but her lashes flickered down, hiding them from him.

'I'm not sure…' she muttered, blushing self-consciously. It was hard to believe she had found enough courage to get the words out.

'You know you don't have to be shy with me any more. The time for that is gone.'

Slowly, nervously, she peeled off her top and jeans. Alessandro watched, absorbed by her body. Grasping her hands, he tugged her down onto the warm, soft rug before the fire. His practised fingers removed her lacy, insubstantial underwear. Pulling her into his arms again, he compressed the fullness of her breasts against the rough warmth of his clothed chest.

'I'm going to make this incredible for you.' Arousal turned his quiet laughter into a throb of anticipation.

Shocked by the power of her body's response, Michelle was excited, too, as fiery sensations over-whelmed her. His kisses plundered still more passion from her mouth while his hands moulded her naked breasts. Teasing her nipples into peaks between his thumb and forefinger, he sent a fizz of arousal straight to the most feminine parts of her body. Cat-like, she arched to meet him. Her teeth grazed his shoulder as she tried to stop herself moaning with pleasure. Her reaction enticed him to increase her torment until she felt dizzy with desire. The way he played her nipples set her alight with passion.

When she realised she was biting him in her desper-ate need to stay silent, she forced her mouth open with an agonised cry. Desperately, her fingers clenched in the yielding luxuriance of the rug beneath their writhing bodies.

Driven half out of his mind by the passion of her response, Alessandro discarded as much of his clothing as he could without releasing her. He couldn't bear to let her go. He could not get enough of her: her perfume, her taste, the feel of her beneath his fingers…

Naked at last, he switched his attention back to the swell of her breasts and their pouting peaks. His lips enclosed one nipple, drawing it into his mouth, where his tongue encircled it. The same raw masculinity sent his hand swooping down her body to part her legs and find the warm heart of her female need.

Michelle's whole body rippled with unexpected feelings of wanton heat. Her fingers slid through Alessandro's hair, keeping his mouth close to her breast as she rode the waves of delight he stirred within her. She could feel the moist excitement of her sex opening like a flower as it responded to his touch.

'Alessandro… Oh, Alessandro…' A voice was calling his name, and it was hers. Michelle was hardly aware her lips were forming the words.

Alessandro paused. He sensed she was on the edge of orgasm, and he wanted his own fulfilment to be part of her soaring enjoyment.

He moved over her easily, his hands gliding over her body to pull her still closer to him. As he thrust, his kisses increased. Michelle rose to meet him, her body searching for something her mind knew little about, but which felt good. So very, very good. Her body stretched, drawing him in with a desperate urgency to hold him as close as possible. Though he fought to control his body, it would not be denied.

The explosion of his orgasm swept Michelle up to heights she had never dreamed existed. Then, as she felt Alessandro pulsing into her with his own release, great swooping waves of pleasure ran through her body as she reached fulfilment in the shelter of his arms.

As she drifted back to earth, his enfolding warmth made her whole being sing with happiness. She was so totally content, even when Alessandro withdrew from her body. She knew now that although she might never keep him, her mind would store the few precious moments when he was totally hers. The memory of him would be hers for ever. The afterglow of their lovemaking brought Michelle the kind of warm satisfaction that had been missing from her life for too long. She revelled in it, watching Alessandro from beneath drooping lashes.

Struggling to keep awake was almost impossible—until she managed to focus sleepily on his expression. He was watching her drifting between wakefulness and sleep. But she could see his eyes were totally lacking in emotion. Once again, Michelle was knocked back. A single tear escaped and ran over the curve of her cheek. Alessandro saw it. He took her in his arms and kissed it away, whispering to her in his own language.

She could not understand what he was saying, but she knew only too well what was making him sound so grim. Marriage vows would bind her and his child to him for ever. He must be warning her what to expect. Total loyalty on her part could expect only occasional fidelity from him.

He might kiss away her tears now—but only for as long as *he* chose…

Alessandro woke with a smile on his face. In seconds it became dread. What on earth had he done? What had possessed him to take her again and again when she had said she wanted to wait? Something wild had overcome his natural gallantry. That was as unforgivable as taking her virginity in the first place. What was it about this woman that made him forget everything except his delight in her body?

He moved his head slightly, and confirmed what the warm, solid presence at his back was telling him. Michelle lay beside him. She was still fast asleep.

'You are a minx and a schemer. I was intending to

wait for our marriage also—what happened to all my good intentions?' he muttered into the cool morning air.

Carefully, so as not to waken her, he managed to look at his watch. It was nearly 7:00 a.m. At some point during the night they had made it as far as his huge double bed. Eventually sated, they had fallen asleep in each other's arms.

Alessandro knew he should get up, forget the night, and turn his attention to the working day. Instead he lingered, gazing down at Michelle. He could hardly bear to abandon her a second time—not after what had happened to trigger all this in the first place. It would have to be done...although not for a few minutes. He wanted time to savour what he was looking at.

The fullness of her breasts was accentuated by the gentle rise and fall of her breathing. She was dead to the world, and it transformed her face. For now she looked totally at peace. Alessandro knew she would be worrying away at something from the moment her eyes opened, so he let her sleep on. The sight pleased him almost as much as his own body's total satisfaction with their lovemaking.

Then she moved slightly.

'Alessandro?'

He leaned forward, trying to catch her first words. Almost in the same instant he realised she was still asleep.

He needed to go, but something kept him at her side. He told himself it was because he could not possibly leave her to wake up alone a second time. Just as he was convincing himself that was the only reason keeping him there, Michelle moved again slightly. The sheet slipped away, leaving the whole of her naked body on show. Now he needed no excuse to linger. He was spellbound—especially when he caught sight of the scene reflected in one of the vast gilt mirrors lining his bedroom.

Tousled and unshaven, he looked like what he was—but Michelle looked like an angel. Totally untroubled in sleep, there was a wild sensuality about her that wouldn't have been out of place in one of the finest Old Masters. It almost stopped his heart. She was totally irresistible. Lifting his hand, he was about to stroke her awake, but hesitated. He knew he mustn't encourage her. It would be unfair to pretend he could be faithful. His father and all his uncles had been serial adulterers. And his mother… Alessandro's face contorted at her shimmering, faithless memory. His heart sank. He had inherited trouble from both sides of his family.

Lying back, he wondered what had happened to his once legendary self-control. This should never have happened. Michelle had wanted to delay sex until their deal was sealed by the marriage ceremony. If she woke to find herself in his bed, she might blame herself for caving in. Despite her willingness…

Silently, he got up and lifted her gently. She only stirred to snuggle more securely in his arms. After carrying her quietly through the villa, he placed her in her own bed. Her whole bedroom was flooded with light, shadowing the gentle curves and hollows of her body. Alessandro watched her, transfixed. In sleep, all her cares had fallen away. She looked so fragile, so utterly desirable. He feasted his eyes on the place where his child was growing, safe and sound. No harm would come to it now, or in the future. *I've got everything completely under control*, he thought with a smile.

Kneeling on the edge of the bed, he kissed the taut, silken skin of her belly. It was so delicious his lips lingered—and felt the unmistakable flutter of a first kick. He waited, desperate to be sure—and there it was again! Michelle murmured something, but when Alessandro turned to her in delight he saw she was still asleep.

His smile vanished. She hadn't said anything about feeling their baby move. The thought struck him that perhaps this was the first time it had happened. He wondered whether to wake her up and ask. But what if it was? As the baby's mother, Michelle should be first to experience it. How could he rob her of her body's best-kept secret?

With agonising care, he got off the bed and pulled the duvet gently over her. Then he backed carefully towards the door, praying the baby would dance her awake right now, so they could share the moment.

It didn't happen.

Alessandro closed the door on her and came to a big decision. However much he wanted to share his joy, he had to keep silent. Michelle must think *she* was the first to feel her baby quicken.

When she woke up in her own bed, and alone, Alessandro's message came through loud and clear to Michelle. *I've got my uses, but nothing can keep me in his bed the whole night long*, she realised bitterly. And when she discovered he had already left the villa for his office in the city, her pain was indescribable. He had satisfied himself, so that was an end of it.

She felt sick. This time it wasn't the baby provoking her nausea; it was its father—and her own behaviour. Last night she had been too lost in sensuality to remember all the pain he had brought her in the past. Now, in the bleak chill of the morning after, she realised all too clearly the reality of life with Alessandro.

Oh, what have I done?

She got unsteadily out of bed and looked at her reflection in the cheval glass on the far side of the room. She had agreed to a marriage of convenience where all the convenience was on Alessandro's side. The vows would only be binding on her.

She walked over to the windows, feeling the Tuscan sun stream over her body like warm honey. The sky still had the soft blush of dawn about it. As she looked down on the intricately cut box edging of the parterre garden, Michelle wondered how many generations of aristocratic husbands had parked their wives in this lonely paradise over the centuries. She thought back to the history lessons she had loved so much at school. Mistresses had fun in town. Wives and children were kept at a safe distance in the country. *I'm not alone. I'll be following in a long tradition*, she thought, trying to come to terms with her situation.

Alessandro had suggested she could turn her back on his generosity and walk away. *That only goes to show he doesn't understand me at all*, Michelle thought. She wrapped her arms around her body and gazed down into the sunlit garden. Her life had been hard before she met him. Losing him and going back to England as a single parent would be impossible. She could never find it in her heart to condemn a baby to the sort of childhood she'd had. The poor little mite deserved everything she could give it. If that meant legally binding herself to Alessandro, then that was what she must do.

The artist she had loved had gone. In his place was a flint-hearted businessman. Both were called Alessandro Castiglione, but one was real, and one was a disguise put on according to his whim. Last night had been a more truthful glimpse of his character. From now on he would consider sex with her as his right and duty, not a lasting pleasure.

A wave of embarrassment and shame engulfed her. It was bad enough to have indulged herself like that, but when she next met Alessandro she'd have to face him knowing she meant so little to him he didn't want her sharing his bed all night. Oh, no doubt he'd be tactful and charming about it, but Michelle knew in her heart that Alessandro was one of those men who should have a neon sign saying 'For one night only' over his bedroom door.

She went into her bathroom. It was a mirrored wonderland, but Michelle could not look herself in the face. What had she been thinking of, giving herself to a man like that in the first place? That question was only too easy to answer. All those stars in her eyes had blinded her to his real character. Alessandro would never be interested in turning their original passion into a lasting love, or for that matter any sort of love at all. Why should he? He must meet wave after wave of classier contacts and more beautiful women every working day.

I might become his wife in name, but I'll never be anything more than a one-night stand for him, she thought bitterly.

When they'd first met he hadn't been looking for

anything more than fun. He'd found it in her. For him, that was all it would ever be—but Michelle now knew the cost to her heart would be almost more than she could bear.

Despite Alessandro's determination to treat marriage as nothing more than a convenience, his mind kept wandering back to Michelle. The Castiglione building in Florence was full of reminders of his home. The boardroom, the dining room and the corridors on the executive floor were all hung with his acrylics and watercolours of the villa and its estate. And taking pride of place on the wall opposite the desk in his office was a life-size study of Michelle at the poolside of Jolie Fleur, worked up from the sketches he had done of her.

If Alessandro was honest, it was the best thing he had ever painted, but he could not bring himself to admit that—even to himself. The more he looked at the canvas, the more he found to dislike in what he had done. He'd been too heavy handed. He hadn't planned properly or taken enough care. The whole thing was emotionally charged—a world away from the measured, bloodless way he conducted business. And it was having a bad effect on him, he realised, as a representative from one of the city's museums felt the need to clear his throat twice before he could drag Alessandro's attention away from the painting.

'And you're an engaged man now!' his elderly client teased him. 'What in the world will your fiancée say when she walks in and sees *that* little peach on display?'

Without once taking his eyes off the painting, Alessandro stood up and crossed his office. He stood within touching distance of the voluptuous curves that were now nourishing his child, gazing at them long and hard.

'She will have no interest in coming here. But you're right. This is far too much of a distraction,' he said brusquely, turning the picture round to face the wall. 'The days of pleasures like that are long gone.'

The thrum of helicopter blades sent all the staff of the Villa Castiglione into a panic. Michelle rushed out onto the upper gallery to see what all the fuss was about. She was just in time to see a helicopter with the House of Castiglione logo descend past the windows. By the time she reached the ground floor Alessandro had neatly settled his craft in the inner courtyard. Ducking from beneath its slowing blades, he met Michelle on the threshold.

'Alessandro! I thought you'd be away for ages!'

'I can see that.' Checking his watch, he looked into her face carefully. 'Didn't you get the list of instructions I left behind? You should be resting at this time.'

'I was—until you arrived. When I heard a helicopter rattling the roof tiles I got scared...'

He snapped his fingers irritably. '*Dannazione!* I warned Security as I flew in. They should have told you.'

Michelle shook her head. 'You've also ordered them to keep the house an oasis of calm for the good of the baby, remember? Security might well have told the house, but the staff would *never* have disturbed my nap. They were probably scared of what you'd do if they woke me. And they would have expected *you* to let me sleep, too,' she finished pointedly.

He grimaced. 'Point taken—it won't happen again anyway. I'm going to be staying here full-time from now on. I've decided to take a short sabbatical from work.'

The announcement puzzled Michelle, but she tried to look on the bright side. While he took a break from business, at least she would always know where he was. Her spirits began to lift as she realised there could be another advantage, too. With all the troubles of commuting and the business day taken off his shoulders, Alessandro might be able to relax. The carefree artist who had swept her off her feet might reappear in her life…

'Oh, good—you'll be able to spend some time in your studio, painting!' she said with relief.

He silenced her with a look. 'What makes you think there will be any time for that? I've got far too much to do—organising everything in time for the arrival of my heir. You should go back to bed. Monsieur Marcel will be here in—' he checked his Rolex '—forty-eight minutes' time, and you'll want to be wide awake to discuss designs for your wedding gown, won't you?'

He dropped a kiss on her brow. Michelle suspected this was for the benefit of the servants, who were all watching and smiling.

'But—shouldn't getting ready for our baby be a joint effort?' she said, one eye on the staff. They made her nervous, despite their kindly expressions.

Alessandro patted her arm. 'It is. Your body is doing all the hard work, I'm making sure everything else runs like clockwork.'

With that, he strode off into his office. Michelle was left to trudge back upstairs alone.

* * *

She didn't have a chance to go back to sleep. Within minutes cars began arriving and doors started banging. People were already arriving for consultations with Alessandro.

Later, as Monsieur Marcel took her measurements and showed her his portfolio of dresses he had designed for celebrities, a maid brought Michelle a timetable for the following day. It was laid out with meetings: dieticians, nursery staff and lifestyle experts were all going to be consulting with her. Michelle had no idea why. Alessandro was so confident *he* would be making all the decisions.

Tired and disappointed, she was beginning to feel like nothing more than an apple tree nourishing a mistletoe baby—or a convenient brood mare. There would be no room in Alessandro's life for her once the baby arrived. Michelle was certain of it. As a person in her own right she might as well not exist. All she could focus on was the way she would be sidelined. She had been so blind! The more she thought about it, the more she realised she had lost the Alessandro she loved long ago. It had happened the first time he walked out on her in France. She couldn't face married life walking on eggshells, waiting to be cast aside again. And this timetable was the end.

Apologising to the dress designer, she leapt up and marched through the villa on a whirlwind tour to find Alessandro. She had never felt so determined to stand up for herself. *He thinks that taking responsibility for my pregnancy means he owns my days as well as my body!* she thought fiercely. She had to get her argument in first—before he distracted her with those come-to-bed eyes and his easy charm.

Those eyes… She wavered.

Her steps slowed and became more hesitant as an image of him danced through her mind. Then she gritted her teeth and marched on with renewed intent. Without Alessandro her life was empty on so many levels—and she resented it. She wanted independence, but life was nothing without him. The more she thought about being a wife in name only, the more trapped she felt.

Righteous fury sent fear and resentment coursing through her veins. When she discovered Alessandro in the villa's vast library, talking to his architect, she was ready to blow. Hearing her familiar light steps, he turned with a smile that would have stopped lava. It had no effect on Michelle. She confronted him, hands on hips.

'I've been looking everywhere for you!'

Alessandro was taken aback by her outburst. The warmth of his smile vanished behind a cloud of suspicion, as he dismissed the man he had been talking to.

'Well, now you've found me. What has happened? What's the matter?'

'Don't start! You've put me off in the past, Alessandro, but you aren't going to do it again!'

'Now, wait a minute, Michelle!'

'No! Let me speak! I can't go on living like this a minute longer! You storm back into my life and drag me off to live behind ten-foot-high walls. My every movement is monitored, but you still can't commit to me. Well, this might be your own personal kingdom, Signor Castiglione, but that doesn't mean you can dictate every second of my life!'

'Are you trying to tell me that you won't like living here?' As cool and collected as ever, Alessandro went over to the iced water dispenser.

'Water! Is that all anyone can ever think of to give me?'

'Some men might smack your bottom, like the spoiled child you are turning out to be,' Alessandro drawled, looking down at her. 'Myself, I prefer a more dignified approach.'

'Me? Spoiled?' Michelle was aghast. 'How can you have the nerve to stand there and accuse me of that when *you're* the one who wants everything his own way!'

'I'm always willing to negotiate.' Alessandro remained totally unfazed. He peeled an absorbent paper coaster from a pile beside the water cooler. Placing it on the highly polished library table, he put the glass of water down.

'Who *are* you, Alessandro?' Michelle asked, exasperated. 'Not the man I met in France, that's for sure! What happened to the gentle, funny man who seduced me in summer?'

Alessandro gazed at her, long and hard. Then he looked away abruptly.

'He became a father. I take my duties and my responsibilities seriously. That's what I'm doing, and so should you, Michelle. The time for fun and games has gone.'

'Some marriage this is going to be,' she retorted.

Alessandro inhaled, long and slow.

'That, of course, is up to you.'

'Are you saying I have a *choice* in all this?'

'There's always a choice,' he said, his voice as coldly insistent as a mountain stream. 'You could put an end to everything right now. Turn and walk away. If you genuinely believe I don't have my child's very best interests at heart, and that you could do better for him by yourself, then I won't stop you.'

His face was totally impassive. Michelle looked into it and believed. He couldn't care less about her. Her life was in ruins, yet he could stand calmly by and give her the chance to make things still worse for herself. If Alessandro was truly so unfeeling towards her, she had nothing left to lose. It made her stake everything on one last, desperate gesture.

'I can't. You know that as well as I do, Alessandro. In your own selfish, twisted way you want this baby every bit as much as I do. The only way I can keep my child safe is by making sure I'm never more than a heartbeat away from it. As far as I'm concerned, that chains me to you tighter and more permanently than any padlock.'

He wheeled away, grasping at the high marble mantelpiece for support. His fist bounced against the cold white stone and his voice had the accuracy of a mason's blade.

'I knew this would happen the moment I let anyone into my life!' he said fiercely. 'It was exactly the same with my—'

He stopped. Pushing himself away from the fireplace, he confronted her. The light of battle was switched off. He glared at her, his chest rising and falling rapidly as his anger boiled away. His face was contorted in the way of someone who had said too much. He was obviously wounded, but Michelle wasn't going to let him get away with it.

'With *who*, Alessandro? All your other girlfriends? Well, pardon me if my heart doesn't exactly bleed for you! I don't have the luxury of being able to compare. You were the first and only man for me.'

She levelled a look of vivid disappointment at him. When he took a step back she tried to feel victorious. Instead she felt nothing but the ache of loss and longing. It pressed tears against her lids and forced badly considered words from her lips.

'And if this is what life with you is going to be like, then I'm better off out of it!'

She turned and blundered blindly for the door, scrabbling past chairs and furniture in her desperation to get away. The only thing more important than escape was the need to feel Alessandro make a commitment to her. She wanted him to reach out, pull her back into her rightful place in his arms and never let her go. Instead he sent nothing after her.

The flood of tears she refused to let him see choked into an indistinct gurgle of grief. 'I'm sorry to have wrecked your master plan!'

She reached the hall, but did not stop. Staff rushed forward with her coat and gloves, but she pushed past them, desperate for the door. Bursting out of the villa, she gasped as cold fresh air seared her lungs. Every breath burned with the rage and disappointment she had been suppressing for so long. Despite her frustration, she was still determined not to cry in front of him. Rushing away from the house, she plunged out into the estate, not caring where she was going.

CHAPTER TWELVE

MICHELLE ran until her legs wouldn't carry her any farther. Finally, despite the cold, she sank down, exhausted. Her resting place, beneath a gnarled olive tree had been sucked dry by its ancient roots. It was as drained as she was.

Like everything and everyone else on this estate, Signor Alessandro Castiglione owned it. *And that includes me*, she thought. It wasn't fair. Her life had never been her own. First her father had pushed her into winning a scholarship. Then when he was killed, her mother had wrecked that future. Only when her mother had died had Michelle managed to get a life. And then she'd met Alessandro.

She wiped a dusty hand across her faced and looked around. Almost all the vast Castiglione estate was visible from this viewpoint. Autumn sunlight sparkled on the metal ladders of men pruning the olive trees. A tractor crawled slowly over the shoulder of a distant hill as an army of grape-pickers moved backwards and forwards, emptying their bags into its trailer. Estate workers were clearly kept hard at it from first light until dusk, bringing in the harvest.

Michelle began to realise they were as tied to boring routine as she had been once upon a time. Alessandro had changed all that for her. He was a good man. Learning about the baby after so long apart had been a shock for him. It was no wonder he'd acted in the way he did. *He's only making the best of it, bringing me here to make sure his child gets a good life.*

Despite her trampled dreams and the cold, despite everything she had been through and everything that was surely to come, Michelle started to laugh. *Oh, poor me! I flew into a rage and sent away a top dress designer, picked a fight with my irresistible soon-to-be husband and ran out into the freezing cold—all because I'm trapped in paradise with nothing to look forward to but the birth of my totally adorable baby!*

Put like that, self-pity was the last thing she should be feeling. Picking herself up, Michelle tried to brush the silver-grey dust from her clothes. She realised her hands were plastered, and then remembered touching her face. Sure enough, she felt powdery streaks. It wouldn't do for anyone to see her like this—crumpled, tearstained and grubby.

She looked around at the paradise she had been finding so hard to appreciate. As her gaze travelled down the hillside she spotted the studio Alessandro had told her about, set in the boundary wall that snaked around the estate.

A smile spread across her face. She knew there would be a sink inside, where she could freshen up. There would be other things, too. Alessandro might not have put up any resistance to her running away, but it hadn't always been like that. There was another side to him—his art. She wanted to glimpse it again, and relive those few tender moments they had shared.

Alessandro's studio was a one-roomed, low-roofed building. All the windows were on the north side, which faced into the estate. This made it totally private. Getting inside was much less trouble than Michelle had expected. Confident in all his security systems, he hadn't bothered to lock the door. Its handle was stiff with disuse, but Michelle persevered. She needed all her strength to work it. There was nothing wrong with the hinges, which swung open smoothly without a sound.

She paused on the threshold. Alessandro's workshop was not a bit like the studio house in France. This place was dark and sad with abandoned dreams. She shivered—and not only because of the cold. This wasn't a place to linger. Turning to leave, she discovered she was in trouble. The door wouldn't open. She had closed it against the wind that threatened to scatter Alessandro's already tumbled papers and artwork. Now it refused to open.

She groaned. If only she hadn't dashed out without picking up her coat and mobile phone! She blew on her hands, but it did no good. There were so many chinks in the old building, and the wicked wind found every one of them. Luckily, as an artist's studio, it wasn't short of rags. Blocking every draught she could find took Michelle's mind off the fact it would soon be dark. Poking around the small single room, she discovered a little oil lamp. Eventually she found a heater, too.

Alessandro had been using it as a table, she noticed disapprovingly.

As she tried to slide the heater out from its hiding place, piles of books, papers and abandoned projects began to shift. She tried to stop the landslide, but it attacked on too many fronts. Although she managed to catch some, sheaves of work flowed past her open arms and slithered to the ground. Her hands were so cold it would take ages to stack it all up again. She decided to warm herself first, and then set to work.

The heater's burners were black with soot, but eventually she got it going. She had done a good job with the draught-proofing too. Within minutes she was beginning to thaw out. Kneeling down on the floor, she began sorting out the paperwork covering the floor. There was no system to any of it. Books and back copies of craft magazines had been heaped up anyhow. Many of them had old receipts or sketches used as bookmarks. It was quite a contrast from Alessandro's great formal library back in the villa!

As she tidied around, Michelle found a packing case filled to the top with all sorts of interesting things. She didn't mean to look, and mostly she didn't have to. Everything was neatly filed in plastic wallets or cardboard covers, with a line or two of description on the front and some dates. The first file she pulled out was dated only a few weeks earlier.

Remembering the old saying 'eavesdroppers hear no good of themselves', she put it back quickly, afraid it might contain something about her. She imagined she would be on safer ground with the volumes of school reports and photographs, further down. She was wrong.

Alessandro had been clever and keen at school, which was more than could be said for either of his parents. She read a dozen variations on the theme of '...*it would be useful to see you both at least once...*'

The Castiglione family might be long on tradition, but they were short on affection. Reading through the paperwork, she discovered that Alessandro had spent virtually all his school holidays marooned in the boarding houses of the best English public schools. That was no life for a child. Michelle burned at the injustices done to him. Curious to see who had inflicted such a sentence, she delved further into the archives.

There were typed letters signed in flowing hands, claiming important business as far afield as Kentucky, Melbourne, London and the South of France. For every apology there was a newspaper clipping dated in Alessandro's writing: photographs of an aristocratic, self-satisfied man at the races, a gaunt supermodel watching Wimbledon from behind enormous designer sunglasses or on the red carpet at Cannes. Michelle scowled. No child of hers was going to suffer absentee parents.

I bet he hated being treated like this, she thought, remembering headlines like *'Poor Little Rich Boy'*, and the press coverage of his abandonment and isolation. *If I go in all guns blazing, accusing him of inflicting the same life on his own child before it's even born, we'll fight and achieve nothing.*

She sat down with her back against the packing case, considering. There had to be another way. When she was a child she'd sat back and taken everything life—or rather her mother—had thrown at her. That had got her nowhere. But arguing with Alessandro was pointless—and painful, too. She had been smothered as a child. Alessandro had been left to fend for himself. With a pang, Michelle realised she had been trying to turn the tables too completely. She wasn't used to independence. It made her heavy handed when it came to getting what she wanted.

As she thought her way around the problem, she began to see a way ahead. Alessandro was a tycoon. Businessmen spent their time negotiating. He was used to that way of working, so she'd learn to do it too. Then she could make sure their baby got a fair share in its father's life. She smiled. A lovely warm glow of satisfaction spread through her. Any minute now she would try to get out again and head back to the villa, ready to apologise and put her new plan into action. But not quite yet…

The studio had warmed up well. *It's almost stuffy*, she thought with a frown. But letting in fresh air would mean cooling the place down. She closed her eyes. It would be a shame to open a window when she'd worked so hard to get the place warm. And taking a nap might stave off the headache that was starting to creep up on her…

Deep in thought, Alessandro rubbed a forefinger back and forth across his upper lip. It was a complete mystery. Michelle had vanished from the face of the earth. The last time he'd seen her she had been storming away from the villa, furious enough to walk all the way to England. Yet no one had seen her leave the estate. He was concerned. Michelle had turned his carefully ordered life on its head, and now she had disappeared.

It wasn't possible. Part of him laughed off the idea of a woman walking out on him. But way down in the deepest corners of his soul another emotion was stirring. It was an overpowering need to know where she was. This was an alien feeling for him. In the past he had secretly felt glad whenever a woman tired of his attitude and flounced away. It had saved him the trouble of ditching her.

Losing Michelle was a completely different prospect. He hadn't expected her to call his bluff. He'd never dreamed she would actually storm out.

And his reaction to what had happened stunned him most of all.

He wanted her back.

Now he came to think of it, he'd actually wanted her back in his life from the moment he'd left her in France.

He stared deep into the flames flickering in the library hearth, remembering. Her wide-eyed nervousness at their first meeting had been delicious. Their midnight talk on the swing-seat had turned out even better. And as for that morning in the pool…

A smile lightened his lips. Firelight danced in his eyes as he thought back over those few happy days. Where had they gone? He thought about the sketches he had made in France, the painting in his office, and the furious work he had done in his studio when he returned home. The images that had captured the raw intensity between them in France…

No one had seen her leave the estate.

It was the clue he needed. Michelle was so like him— they both craved solitude, yet deep down shared a need for security. She would have gone to the one place inside the estate boundary where Alessandro needed to go himself. Now all he had to do was fetch her back.

Michelle might resent having to accept his help, but her independence and stability was exactly what *he* needed to experience right now. Striding out of the house with new determination, he went off to find her.

The evening was brittle with cold. Plunging out of the villa, Alessandro entered a shadowy world of starlight. Owls in the valley sent out mournful wails and quavers. He barely noticed. Covering the distance between the house and his studio in less than ten minutes, his footsteps crunched on the gritty path.

Breasting the hill, any chill vanished instantly in his warm glow of satisfaction at being proved right. A feeble orange light stood out against the darkness. Alessandro stopped to savour the moment. It was then he wished he'd brought his jacket. Wrapping Michelle up in it to carry her home would have felt so good… The thought made him smile as he set off down the hillside.

His good humour didn't falter until there was no reply to his knock at the studio door. He tried again.

'It's me, Michelle. I've come to say—' The word stuck in his throat.

She had accused him of being a different man. If she still wanted the man who had seduced her in France, then he wanted to change back. But apologising at the top of his voice through solid oak was a challenge too far.

He tried the door. It wouldn't budge. Annoyed, he looked through the window. The light was fading fast, and he could hardly see anything in the growing gloom—except the old heater he'd been using as a temporary table.

The last time he'd lit that, the pounding headache

he'd developed had been enough of a warning that it wasn't working properly.

But now it was standing in the centre of the room.

There was no time to think. Alessandro kicked the door down, recoiling at the thick, suffocating atmosphere. The little oil lamp flared in the sudden rush of fresh air. In its ghastly light he saw Michelle, slumped against a packing case. Taking a deep breath he darted into the airless studio and pulled her outside.

The shock of being so roughly handled combined with the cold night air brought her back to life with a groan.

'Oh…my head…'

'*Idiota!*' Alessandro struck his forehead with the heel of his hand.

'Hold on…' Grabbing at the flotsam and jetsam of their last argument, Michelle dog-paddled back to consciousness. 'Don't start calling me names—'

'I was talking to myself. I let you run off, and I thought I'd lost you—' Alessandro began desperately, but words were no longer enough. He pulled her into his arms, hugging her so hard it squeezed nearly all the breath out of her lungs. 'Oh, Michelle…'

She was confused, but she didn't care. Alessandro was here, she was in his arms, and in her mind there was only one thing more important than that.

'The baby…' she wailed.

'No, Michelle—I'm more worried about *you*!'

The intensity of Alessandro's desperate cry brought them both to their senses. They stared at each other, white-faced. It was an impulsive show of emotion neither had expected. Desperate to distract Michelle from his slip, Alessandro started to lower her to the ground. Changing his mind, he took a firmer grip on her, and fastened a manfully flinty gaze on the horizon.

'That is…what I *meant* to say was—you have to be OK, Michelle, if our—*your*—baby—I mean, my *heir*—is going to have any chance of survival.'

No matter how many alterations he made to stiffen his story, Alessandro was determined to the end. Michelle searched his face, trying to spot some glimmer of tenderness behind his stony facade.

Still trying to cover his tracks, Alessandro dragged his feelings onto higher moral ground. 'Didn't you have the sense to know that old lamp and the heater might use up all the oxygen? You could have killed yourself!'

The breath caught in his throat, and his expression changed abruptly. His eyes became dark points of pain. Michelle watched as some other, far worse conclusion contorted his features.

'Or is that what you intended? After the way you stormed out of the library?'

There was no pretence about his voice now. Only pure dread.

For a long time Michelle could not answer. She shut her eyes, unable to bear the horror in his gaze. How could he possibly think such a thing? Tears couldn't wash away the pounding pain from her head, and her throat was raw. Eventually she managed to move her head, first to the left, then the right.

'Never.' The single word whispered into the cold, clean air between them. 'I couldn't bear the thought I might never see you again.'

After she said that, Alessandro was so quiet for so long that she opened her eyes. He was looking down at her, and his face was transformed. Words came out eventually, through a haze of disbelief.

'After all I've done? Taking away your independence and bringing you to a place where you don't even speak the language?'

Her eyes never left his as she took hold of his hands and squeezed them between her own. 'You only did it because you cared for our baby—in a way that no one ever cared for you when you were young.'

His lines of concern for her deepened, then his beautiful dark eyes flicked towards the studio. 'You found the press cuttings?'

She nodded. 'And that isn't all. I read some of the correspondence, too, Alessandro. It was wrong of me, but I couldn't help it. I'm so sorry.'

'Don't apologise. I've read plenty of things I shouldn't have in the past—'

'No—I mean I'm sorry that you went through such torture,' she interrupted him, finding renewed strength at the memory of all those icily formal letters. 'Now I can see why you are so absorbed in our baby.'

'If you picked that up from the personal things,' he said, his eyes guarded, watching her for any clue to her reaction, 'then the newspaper articles about my parents must have told you all you need to know about me.'

She gazed at him, trying to fathom meaning from his pained expression. Slowly she shook her head. 'No…all I saw was a bewildered little boy treated as nothing more than a bargaining chip. The two people in the world you should have been able to trust and rely on to put you first seemed to spend their whole lives trampling over each other in their search for publicity.'

'That's why it is always such a relief to escape from the public eye and come here, to the Villa Castiglione.'

'Then surely that's all the more reason for you to make the effort to stay here more often?' she said quietly.

'You're the last person who should be encouraging me.' He gave a mirthless laugh. 'Why would a treasure like you want to spend time with someone who has adulterous genes on both sides of his family?'

'Adulterous genes?' Michelle erupted in laughter, before clapping a hand to her throbbing head. 'What in the world are they?'

'Neither of my parents had it in them to be faithful.'

Michelle narrowed her eyes. 'Why go looking for trouble? You work hard, and all the arrangements you're making for this baby show how selfless and generous you can be. That makes you the complete opposite of your parents, from what I've read about them. I certainly work hard not to take after *my* mother. She was a hypochondriac. That's why I really hated it when you saw me being sick. I like to keep my troubles to myself.' She patted her tummy thoughtfully.

He slipped his arms around her again. Keeping her warm felt *so* good. 'It was no trouble. I'm responsible for the way you are feeling. I want to help.'

His concern was so genuine she couldn't help smiling. 'Thanks, but don't worry. It's my problem! I can't stand anyone seeing me ill. I'm convinced they'll think I'm putting it on, because that's the way Mum always—' Her smile faltered. 'Alessandro...'

He was alert instantly. 'What is it?'

She grabbed his hand and pulled it towards her.

Alarmed, he wrenched it free and started fumbling for his mobile. 'It's OK—I'll ring for an ambulance—'

'There's no need!' With one hand Michelle snatched his phone, while the other pressed his palm hard against her body, low down. He looked deep into her eyes, questioning. She returned his look with one of distant concentration, moving his hand around to find exactly the right spot.

'There! Did you feel that?' She looked up at him earnestly.

Alessandro had wondered if he would be able to act surprised when Michelle first felt their baby move. He needn't have worried. After a struggle to find any words at all, he managed.

'It's...the baby...*our* baby,' he said with dawning wonder. 'Michelle...I don't know what to say. I want to pick you up and carry you home to keep you both safe for ever, but I suppose you won't want me to mollycoddle you.'

'From now on you can do as much mollycoddling as you like,' she smiled. 'You'll get no complaints from me.'

'Do you mean that?'

'I've never meant anything more in my whole life.'

'But...'

Emotions flitted across his face as he tried to take in what she had said.

'After all I've done to you?'

'After all you've done *for* me.' She reached up and touched his face. He closed his eyes as their joined hands made slow, gentle movements over the place where she was keeping his child safe and secure.

'My parents acted as a terrible warning to me, but

I've gone too far the other way. They both lived life at a thousand kilometres an hour. Neither was faithful, and both spent their time in the search for celebrity. They prized only things that seemed shallow and short-lived to me. I grew up determined to do things differently in every way I could. But there's one point where both my father and I touch. We both produced an heir for the Castiglione family by accident. The difference is, I'm going to take full responsibility for my child. And for you, *cara mia*. I am going to succeed where my father failed.'

He spoke with such quiet authority Michelle knew he would.

'And that's why my pregnancy is so important to you.'

The warmth of his hold on her fingers reminded her of the heady times they had shared. She wanted to tell him how happy she was, but now was not the time. Her own pleasure was unimportant beside this chance for him to open his soul.

'I don't want conflict and disappointment in my child's life. I want everything to be perfect.'

Michelle thought back to the way he had made that helicopter land precisely in the right place on the lawn of Jolie Fleur.

'I think parenthood might mean making compromises,' she said diplomatically. 'I want our baby to be happy, not perfect. It will have two parents on call all the time, and plenty of space to run and play. That's a far better start in life than lots of children get. Myself, I would have settled for a chance to be my own person when I was little, and not have to live up to someone else's expectations.'

Alessandro smiled and kissed her. His hold on her changed subtly as he caressed her waist, encircling it with his hands to bind her body to his. Then he pulled her into his arms and held her tight.

'From now on that's exactly what you'll have, Michelle—the chance to be yourself. I am going to spend my life making sure you are never sidelined, or lonely, or left out again. That's a promise.'

The expression in his eyes told her she was safe in his heart, now and for ever. Lifting her gently into his arms for the journey home, he kissed her more tenderly than he had ever done before.

'I believe you.' She smiled.

0509_SC_01/06

*More passion,
more seduction,
more often...* ★

Modern™ and Modern Heat™ available twice a month from August 2009!

◎ 6 glamorous new books
1st Friday of every month

◎ 6 more glamorous new books
3rd Friday of every month

Still with your favourite
authors and the same
great stories! ★

Find all the details at:

www.millsandboon.co.uk/makeover

★

◎™ MILLS & BOON®

★

0609/01a

MILLS & BOON

MODERN

On sale 3rd July 2009

THE GREEK TYCOON'S BLACKMAILED MISTRESS
by Lynne Graham

Dark and utterly powerful, Aristandros Xenakis wants revenge –
to see her niece, naïve Ella must become his mistress!

RUTHLESS BILLIONAIRE, FORBIDDEN BABY
by Emma Darcy

Notorious Fletcher Stanton is determined never to take a
wife – but now his inexperienced mistress Tamalyn is
pregnant with his forbidden baby...

CONSTANTINE'S DEFIANT MISTRESS
by Sharon Kendrick

Greek billionaire Constantine Karantinos wants his heir. He
summons Laura to Greece, but his child's mother is less dowdy
and more wilful than he remembers...

THE SHEIKH'S LOVE-CHILD
by Kate Hewitt

When Lucy arrives in the desert kingdom of Biryal, Sheikh
Khaled has changed into a harder, darker man than before. But
they're inextricably bound – he is the father of her son!

THE BOSS'S INEXPERIENCED SECRETARY
by Helen Brooks

For the first time, awkward Kim feels desired! But she must
resist, for her powerful playboy boss Blaise will never offer
her anything more than a temporary affair...

Available at WHSmith, Tesco, ASDA, and all good bookshops
www.millsandboon.co.uk

0609/01b

MILLS & BOON

MODERN

On sale 3rd July 2009

RUTHLESSLY BEDDED, FORCIBLY WEDDED
by Abby Green

Ruthless millionaire Vincenzo seduced Ellie and cruelly discarded her. But she's now pregnant! The Italian will claim her again…as his bride!

THE DESERT KING'S BEJEWELLED BRIDE
by Sabrina Philips

Kaliq Al-Zahir A'zam was outraged when Tamara Weston rejected his marriage proposal. Now Tamara will model his royal jewels – and deliver to him the wedding night he was denied…

BOUGHT: FOR HIS CONVENIENCE OR PLEASURE?
by Maggie Cox

Needing a mother for his orphaned nephew, magnate Nikolai tracks Ellie down to make her his unwillingly wedded wife!

THE PLAYBOY OF PENGARROTH HALL
by Susanne James

Fleur would never make a one-night mistress – but she could be the mistress of Pengarroth Hall – if only Sebastian can overcome his allergy to marriage…

THE SANTORINI MARRIAGE BARGAIN
by Margaret Mayo

Zarek Diakos has decided Rhianne's wasted as his secretary. He's in need of a bride: under the warm Santorini sun he'll show Rhianne it's a position she can't refuse!

Available at WHSmith, Tesco, ASDA, and all good bookshops
www.millsandboon.co.uk

0609/05a

MILLS & BOON
BY REQUEST®
3
NOVELS ONLY
£5.49

On sale
3rd July 2009

In July 2009
Mills & Boon present
two bestselling collections,
each featuring three
fabulous romances
by favourite authors...

His Contract Bride

Featuring

The Marriage Proposition by Sara Craven
The Borghese Bride by Sandra Marton
The Bride Price by Day Leclaire

Available at WHSmith, Tesco, ASDA, and all good bookshops
www.millsandboon.co.uk

0609/05b

**On sale
3rd July 2009**

MILLS & BOON
BY REQUEST
3
NOVELS ONLY
£5.49

Don't miss
out on these
fabulous
stories!

Hired: A Bride for the Boss

Featuring

The Playboy Boss's Chosen Bride by Emma Darcy
The Boss's Urgent Proposal by Susan Meier
The Corporate Marriage Campaign by Leigh Michaels

Available at WHSmith, Tesco, ASDA, and all good bookshops
www.millsandboon.co.uk

WEB/M&B/RTL

MILLS & BOON®
Pure reading pleasure™

www.millsandboon.co.uk

◎ All the latest titles

◎ Free online reads

◎ Irresistible special offers

And there's more...

◎ Missed a book? Buy from our huge discounted backlist

◎ Sign up to our FREE monthly eNewsletter

◎ eBooks available now

◎ More about your favourite authors

◎ Great competitions

Make sure you visit today!

www.millsandboon.co.uk

FREE!
2 Books
and a surprise gift!

We would like to take this opportunity to thank you for reading this Mills & Boon® book by offering you the chance to take TWO more specially selected titles from the Modern™ series absolutely FREE! We're also making this offer to introduce you to the benefits of the Mills & Boon® Book Club™—

- ★ **FREE home delivery**
- ★ **FREE gifts and competitions**
- ★ **FREE monthly Newsletter**
- ★ **Exclusive Mills & Boon Book Club offers**
- ★ **Books available before they're in the shops**

Accepting these FREE books and gift places you under no obligation to buy, you may cancel at any time, even after receiving your free shipment. Simply complete your details below and return the entire page to the address below. You don't even need a stamp!

YES! Please send me 2 free Modern books and a surprise gift. I understand that unless you hear from me, I will receive 4 superb new titles every month for just £3.19 each, postage and packing free. I am under no obligation to purchase any books and may cancel my subscription at any time. The free books and gift will be mine to keep in any case.

P9ZEF

Ms/Mrs/Miss/Mr ....Initials ....

Surname ....**BLOCK CAPITALS PLEASE**

Address ....

....

....Postcode ....

Send this whole page to:
UK: FREEPOST CN81, Croydon, CR9 3WZ

Offer valid in UK only and is not available to current Mills & Boon Book Club subscribers to this series. Overseas and Eire please write for details. We reserve the right to refuse an application and applicants must be aged 18 years or over. Only one application per household. Terms and prices subject to change without notice. Offer expires 31st August 2009. As a result of this application, you may receive offers from Harlequin Mills & Boon and other carefully selected companies. If you would prefer not to share in this opportunity please write to The Data Manager, PO Box 676, Richmond, TW9 1WU.

Mills & Boon® is a registered trademark owned by Harlequin Mills & Boon Limited.
Modern™ is being used as a trademark. The Mills & Boon® Book Club™ is being used as a trademark.